LIGHTS BURNING BLUE

LIGHTS BURNING BLUE

ANDREW CULLUM

Cover image by Fernando

Matador
9 Priory Business Park,
Wistow Road, Kibworth Beauchamp,
Leicestershire. LE8 0RX
Tel: 0116 279 2299
Email: books@troubador.co.uk
Web: www.troubador.co.uk/matador
Twitter: @matadorbooks

ISBN 978 1784625 214

British Library Cataloguing in Publication Data.
A catalogue record for this book is available from the British Library.

Printed and bound in the UK by TJ International, Padstow, Cornwall
Typeset in 11pt Aldine401 BT by Troubador Publishing Ltd, Leicester, UK

Matador is an imprint of Troubador Publishing Ltd

For Jackie
who knows me better than anyone,
and for Sam and Sarah
who have theatre in their blood.

BROOKLYN

"That's right. Brooke. Like a stream."

I'd just arrived in the village at my digs and my landlady asked what I like to be called.

My name needs some explaining: I was christened Brooklyn, and before you ask, no, I'm not American. My parents spent some time in America in the early 1990s; a last expensive holiday before they planned to have a family. The result of their planning was me, except that I happened quite quickly, and I'm pretty sure that I was named after the place where I was conceived: Brooklyn.

"But it's such a pretty name!" Mum says. "You've got two girls' names rolled into one: Brook... Lynn." I guess she has a point, and on the whole I'm glad that my parents hadn't conceived me while they'd been in Hackensack.

To keep life as simple as possible, most people call me Brooke. Everyone that is except Dad, who always calls me Brooklyn (I think my name was his idea), and Scott, who hit it off straightaway with Dad when I introduced him last summer. Anyway, both Brooke Shields and Brooke Adams seem to have done OK in my chosen profession.

It was a Sunday night in late February and already I was wondering if I'd done the right thing. Scott and I had moved into a flat in North London only six months ago. The prospect of not seeing him for six weeks made me feel sad just thinking about it. But work was work and, as a recent drama school graduate who still hadn't managed to do any real acting work in an entire year, I'd begun to feel that 'beggars can't be choosers'.

So I kissed a tear-streaked goodbye to Scott at Waterloo and started the journey to Dorset. One of those journeys where I couldn't settle to anything; just watching the world go by through the window. The papers were full of some story about a murder being committed not far from where I'd be staying. I picked up a copy someone had left behind. There was a picture of a girl about my age who went missing after a night out and was found dead in a wood. I didn't read much of it. Too depressing. Especially with the grief that Mum had given me about not walking back on my own late at night, blah blah blah yatter yatter yatter.

I caught a taxi from Bournemouth out to Cranton Overleigh. Fifteen quid! As we drove through Port St Catherine along the Seafront I had my first real-life glimpse of the Edwardian Palace Theatre, and felt the familiar longing that all actors have; to play in a proper theatre in a proper season. The show I would be working on was being financed by the Edwardian Palace, but would rehearse six miles out of town in Cranton Oh, as the locals called it. Then, having opened in Cranton Overleigh in just two weeks' time, we would tour to a mixture of schools and village halls without ever once playing at the Edwardian Palace. I could still use the prestigious name on my CV though.

The taxi brought me to 32 Claxton Parade, which was to be my home for six weeks. A large house set back from the road. My room was at the very top of the house with a window looking out onto part of the roof. There was a large double bed, handy if Scott could come and stay for a weekend, a recess in the wall with a clothes rail and hangers to serve as a wardrobe, a chest of drawers with a mirror, and a rocking chair with a large teddy bear.

Unpacking had taken all of ten minutes. Underwear in the top drawer. Tee shirts in the bottom one, and anything that would hang up was now doing just that in the recessed wardrobe. I sat in the rocking chair and hugged the teddy bear. My landlady, who was in her late fifties and was called Beth Churchill, had told me that the bear had belonged to her niece and was called Mr Tibbs. Mr Tibbs smelled of ancient stuffing and dusty fur and I felt an odd mix of homesickness and comfort. A bit like I do when I look at old photographs of Mum and Dad and me on holiday when I was a kid, when earning a living wasn't something that I needed to worry about.

I heard a sound outside the door, soft footsteps on the carpet just before a knock at the door. It was Beth. "How are you settling in?" she asked as she peeped tentatively round the door. "Here, I've brought your drink."

"That's very kind," I said. Beth had asked me if I wanted tea, coffee or a glass of wine. No-brainer. A large glass of red wine stood on the tray with a plate of thick slabs of Scottish shortbread.

"I thought this would help you to unwind," she said, and then asked: "So you start work tomorrow?"

"Yes, first thing." I took a mouthful of wine. "Thanks for this. Just what I need."

"You're welcome. Help yourself to anything you need for breakfast in the morning. I'll be around anyway, but just make yourself at home. So… what play are you working on?"

"*Richard III*."

"And which part do you play?"

I took a large pull at my drink to hide my disappointment. "None of them. I'm stage-managing."

"Oh I see… Oh well, never mind dear," said Beth. "I must get on… I'll leave you to it. See you in the morning. Don't worry about bringing the glass down just yet. Leave it until the morning."

She gave a favourite-auntie smile and went back downstairs.

Why did I feel slightly ashamed of the fact that my first real job since leaving college was stage-managing? It's an important job. Vital in fact, and it can be a very rewarding and challenging career. Except in my case I didn't really want to do it ("*Oh well, never mind dear*") – I wanted to act. Always have. Anything less feels like a bit of a failure, even despite the fact that stage-managing was a lot better than trying to interest passing shoppers in cavity wall insulation.

I'd applied for this job half-hoping that I wouldn't get it but telling myself that all experience was valuable. Then as it turned out, the director knew the stage management tutor from my college, Duncan Ward, who recommended me. Thank you Duncan. Hope I don't let you down.

I ate the shortbread and drained the red wine in a couple of luxurious swallows. Hardy's, I thought, impressed by my own sophistication. Probably a Shiraz: full-bodied with a hint of oak and peppery notes. I like to read the labels when I'm choosing a bottle from the Costcutter shop, so give me a break OK?

ARCHIE

The view from the kitchen window hasn't changed much in eighty years. The bushes around the sides of the old hall have become fuller, then have been cut back, and then have grown again, but apart from that the view probably hasn't altered since 1760, when according to the stone over the door, Cranton Overleigh Village School had been built.

The large rhododendron bush near the large, paint-peeled door stirred gently in the morning breeze. I remember that being planted. It would be just ten years ago. I had just had my big birthday party.

The older you get, the more your life shrinks. I'm not as fit as I used to be and simple things like getting going in the morning and having breakfast are sometimes too much of an effort. So I take my time with life's little pleasures. Like looking out of the window and remembering.

The Hall has been part of my life for a long time. When I was a pupil here when it was a school, the head teacher had been Miss Beck. A tall, severe-looking woman, who lived in the house which I now own. My house is only about ten yards away from the hall, and had been built originally for the head teacher and his or her family. Miss Beck lived here with her sister. When I was young I'd thought of them as two of the old ladies of the parish. Looking back, I suspect that they were only in their mid-fifties.

Cranton Overleigh still retains a lot of charm. The hall, now given the grand name of the Cranton Overleigh Institute, the Red Lion pub and the parade of eighteenth century houses near the green, where the old village pump still stands like a forgotten sentry, have all been photographed over the years and sold as postcards in Bateman's grocery shop.

I'm looking out of my window and wondering what to be at. I don't eat breakfast any more. Never seem to feel hungry. Part of getting old I suppose. I'm expecting Old Bill to come along and say hello. He usually does and I don't want to miss him.

Today the weather is much as it was when I brought Sheelagh here. We were down for the weekend, from London. I'd just left the Navy and had been working in Fleet Street. I don't even remember why. Just the need for a job I suppose. I was young and game for anything. On my first day Hamilton showed me to my desk.

"Do you type, Archie?" he asked.

"I think so," I said, feeling very ill-prepared.

"Learn quickly or get another job," said Hamilton, and waddled off. I lasted there about a year. Sheelagh and I had been married only a few months and we had ideas of 'starting again' somewhere new.

Sheelagh wanted to see the village where I'd grown up and one chilly Saturday afternoon we'd walked past the large wooden gate at the end of the path and noticed the *For Sale by Private Auction* sign nailed to the gatepost.

Somehow we managed to get enough money together to buy it, and to persuade our bank manager that Sheelagh's idea to run the hall as a theatre producing a weekly repertoire of summer shows was financially viable.

I knew nothing of the theatre, or of theatre people, but Sheelagh did, and for many years we did quite good business. Agatha Christie, Noel Coward, Bernard Shaw. They had been just names to me, but Sheelagh changed me from a rather over-earnest ex-Navy man into a theatre producer.

All that was years ago. Many years since Sheelagh's obituary in *The Stage*, and her memorial service at the Actors' Church.

After that The Hideaway Theatre faded away slowly. The life had gone out of the place, and I was no longer a young man. Now it's just a village hall with a posh name: The Cranton Overleigh Institute. The sort of name that only a village hall committee could think up.

Jumble sales, whist drives, scout troops all put in an appearance from time to time. One time when the scout troop were off for their summer camp they were loading up their vans with two-man canoes. The boats lay on the small patch of grass outside my front door like hollowed-out torpedoes. Nice lads. I enjoyed telling them a thing or two about boats.

Sometimes there are theatre shows in the old hall: The Cranton Overleigh Players. Usually three nights in March. Sometimes we've had a touring professional group. I've heard the actors talking while they have a fag break outside the hall door.

"This used to be a pro theatre," they say. I never go over. Never see the shows. Not anymore.

Still no sign of Old Bill. Beth won't be popular if she hasn't let him out.

BROOKLYN

When I awoke next morning I wondered where I was. From my bedroom there was no sound of traffic. Very different to North London. Also, at just after seven on a grey February morning it was still quite dark. What light there was, was struggling to get around the heavy curtains.

I silenced the alarm on my iPhone and switched on Radio 4 on the small portable radio. There's something comforting about Radio 4 in the mornings. Scott disagrees, he likes to listen to Radio 1. Says it helps him to wake up. For me, it's a reminder of home. Of Mum and Dad cooking breakfast. Part of the soundtrack of my childhood.

Stop it, I told myself. I'd felt pretty low last night. Scott had called and we'd spoken for half an hour. His phone was provided as part of his job and calls were, in effect, free. Mine was on a monthly contract. As many texts as you need but only an hour's worth of talk-time. Not enough when you're away from home. Not enough when you've only been with the man in your life for less than a year.

Scott and I had met while I was working a temp job in the city. I'd been out of college for about a month and was still living in the bedsit in Kensington where I'd lived for my finals. No matter what your dreams and ambitions, you still have to pay the rent. So while waiting for a break I signed on at Office Angels, and they sent me to Baxter Kendrick as a temp. Some sort of mutual assurance company. I don't know. I had a mind-numbing job in accounts. For some reason the company were happy to pay me to sit at a computer all day entering details of their representatives' expense claim sheets. I devised a strategy for getting through the day and dealing with the crushing boredom: Every hour I'd go for a walk. People would think I was on my way to the photocopier, to the ladies', or to get a coffee. Sometimes I'd come back with a plastic cup of water, but the main thing was just to get away from my desk for a few moments. One day I was in the small kitchen looking at the drinks machine, which stood there like a bloated filing cabinet. The uninspiring choices were tea, tea with milk, tea with extra milk, coffee black, coffee white, coffee extra white, hot chocolate, and one button for extra sugar if you really wanted to be buzzing with energy all day.

I became aware of someone standing behind me.

"I wouldn't, Brooklyn," said a voice; "they all taste disgusting."

I turned round to face a man about my own age. Nice-looking. China blue eyes, fairish hair. I felt myself blushing. I'd noticed him before. Or rather, I'd noticed him notice me. That sounds arrogant. It's not meant to. When you're twenty-three and female you get used to guys checking you out. On the tube, in the street. You don't need to be a babe. I'm just ordinary. It happens.

The accounts section at Baxter Kendrick was huge. My hourly walks would usually take me on a longish, vaguely circular tour round the building. Out of Accounts, through Human Resources, and then past the IT section. I'd been there for about three days when I began to notice that 'Blondie', as I'd started to think of him, would look over as I passed. I hadn't responded. I was only just out of college; for all I knew, any day I could get a job on a theatre tour and disappear to God knows where.

I smiled. "Just felt I needed a caffeine kick," I said, just for something to say.

Blondie smiled. "I'm Scott," he said, "and what's in there might contain caffeine but I wouldn't recommend it."

I smiled, went to introduce myself, stopped when I remembered that he somehow already knew my name, and instead I heard myself whimper, "Nice to meet you."

"So… would you like a coffee?" said Scott.

Now, I believe in saying what you want; but I wasn't prepared for such a speedy chat-up line.

"Er… Yes… OK… that'd be nice. I'm not doing anything after work, so…" I trailed off.

Scott looked puzzled, and was looking at me as though he wasn't quite following me. His eyes held mine and then he laughed.

"No," he chuckled, "I mean would you like some real coffee instead of the slop that comes out of that machine?" He held up a cafetière and a packet of Douwe Egberts. "I bring in my own."

I felt myself blush to my hair roots. "Oh… yes please… thanks… sorry."

Then we both laughed.

Last night after speaking with Scott I'd sat for about half an hour. I was trying hard to feel positive. I'd got a job. OK, so it's not an acting job, but it's a job. In theatre. Last week I'd been handing out leaflets outside Tesco's. "Hi, can I just have few minutes of your time to talk about how you can save ten per cent on your heating bills?" Answers to that varied from polite smiles to deliberate ignorance and even the occasional muttered "Fuck off." At least this would be better than that.

I miss Scott. I want to be in the West End, the National, the RSC; on tour somewhere – not Deputy Stage Manager on some crappy small-scale *Richard III*. Come to think of it, was I even the DSM? On a larger-scale job, the running of the show from the desk, cueing lights and sound, would be the DSM's job, but on this very small-scale show, basically I had to do everything, even making the tea. What Dad would call a general dogsbody.

"Stop it," I said out loud and started to get into bed. *This is it*, I thought matter-of-factly. *This is the reality of ambition. Unless you get very lucky, this is what the acting life is going to be like.* I gave myself what I hoped was an encouraging smile in the mirror on the dressing table by my bed, whispered "Night-night" to Mr Tibbs, and turned out the light.

***

"Morning Brooke, sleep well?" said Beth as I appeared in the kitchen.

"Yes thanks," I said, and meant it. The fresh air with a hint of the sea, the long journey and I suppose the loneliness of last night, had meant I'd dropped off very quickly.

I recoiled involuntarily as something wet touched my hand, and then I smiled. A rather old black Labrador was looking up at me with soulful eyes.

"Hello, aren't you lovely?" I said. He was nuzzling my hand. I stroked his head. His eyes had a milky look to them, and the close hairs around his mouth were flecked with grey.

Beth gave a happy chuckle. "You'll tire of that before he does. He loves attention, don't you boy?" she patted his back as she came past and went into the hall. "Do help yourself to anything you'd like for breakfast."

"Thanks. I'll just have a bit of cereal if that's OK; I'll do some shopping today and get some stuff of my own in."

That was one of the first things on my list of things to do: find a local shop and buy some supplies. Beth was suddenly serious. "Brooke, I don't want to worry you, but you won't be coming back late, will you?"

"No," I said, surprised.

Beth attempted a light tone that I could tell she did not feel. "Ever since last week. I mean the murder…" she broke off. "I'm sure you saw it on the news."

The newspaper on the train. The photographs of the girl who looked a bit like me. "Yes," I said, "of course. It was in this area wasn't it?"

Beth nodded gravely. "Just behind the Institute. In the woods. At least, that's where she was found."

"Yes," I said, stuck for words, and then for something to say, I asked, "Where's that? I'm in the village hall."

Beth fixed me with sad, Mummy's-got-something-serious-to-say eyes, and said, "That's the same place. The village hall is the Institute."

Great. First day of rehearsals in Crapton Ovary or whatever it's called, and I find out there's a psycho lurking in the woods.

I poured some Shreddies, and as I munched them in glum silence, the dog looked wisely up at me. I was anxious to get to the hall early on my first day. I finished my breakfast and went upstairs to clean my teeth. Breakfast cereal; why do I bother? Bits of cardboard with milk, and then when you clean your teeth and spit into the sink, the cardboard has become tiny brown fragments. Gross.

***

It was one of those very bright, early spring days. I walked across the green that separated Claxton Parade from Sea Lion

Street, which according to Google Maps would lead me to the Cranton Overleigh Institute after about half a mile. Either side of the road were fairly ordinary houses. Nothing much to look at, and before long I came to a village green with an old, hand-operated water pump. A pub, The Red Lion. A One Stop shop. No sign of anything claiming to be an institute.

I glanced again at my iPhone. It should be here. I walked over the road to where a large wooden gate was already open on a short drive leading up to the village hall which now loomed in front of me.

On the apex of the roof there still remained the stone frame which would have once held a bell, and a date: 1760. The bell itself had gone. Probably to help fight Hitler all those years ago; or been sold, or nicked by pikeys for the scrap value. But no, this was nice, sedate Dorset, not London.

To my right was a neglected-looking cottage. Dark green paint peeling from the door and window frames. As I passed by, I noticed the door of the cottage was half-open. It had a dead, empty feeling about it. I walked over to the front door of the Village Hall, and there on the door was a typewritten sheet in a plastic bag. *Cranton Overleigh Institute*, and the name and number of one Martin Helgin, keyholder. I was early by about half an hour. I would have to wait.

ARCHIE

"Used to be a pro theatre," those actors said on their fag break.Yes, it did. And a very good one. Sheelagh had chosen the plays and I'd hired the actors and made sure the place made a profit. We made a good team. She was the artist, I the businessman. I expected people to pull their weight. Got rid of a few that didn't over the years. I didn't mind getting rid of people. Sometimes it just had to be done.

The Cranton Overleigh Players. Amateurs. It's good that the place is still used as a theatre, but badly built sets and lines learnt just in time for the dress rehearsal was not Sheelagh's idea of theatre. Or mine. And who wants to go to a pantomime in March anyway?

I heard movement just outside. Bill? I walked to the door, which I always leave open now. No, it wasn't Bill. Where had he got to? It was a young girl carrying a briefcase and looking at a funny handheld gadget that looked like one of those calculator things the youngsters all seem to have. She was wearing jeans and a dark, waist-length jacket. I gave her a wave through the open door, but she didn't see me. I watched her through the window; saw her try the door to the hall. Locked of course. When Sheelagh and I had been in charge it would have been open. Always. People could go in, buy tickets; pick up leaflets for the forthcoming shows. Sheelagh always said there was nothing so disappointing as a closed theatre. They should be welcoming places, full of the promise of fun. The girl turned towards me. She was twenty yards away from me but my eyesight is still good. She was quite pretty. Dark hair cut in a 20s-style bob that gave her face an elfin quality. A bit like Sheelagh when I first met her.

BROOKLYN

Five minutes had gone by and it felt like forever. I'd started to run out of things to look at. I sensed that there was more to the hall out the back than was immediately apparent from the front. Peering through the small window next to the door it was clear that beyond the lobby, which still featured an old, ornate wooden box office, there was a decent-sized hall. I'd heard that this place had once been a professional theatre, but now was just a village hall. Arts Council cuts perhaps.

Just then I saw a familiar figure. Beth's dog, the old black Labrador, came lumbering up the path towards me. He didn't see me; somewhat to my relief. I thought at first that he had followed me. He stopped by the porch of the house just across the path and waited by the slightly open door, looking inside. I watched, expecting him to turn towards me. Instead he stayed motionless and appeared to be listening.

ARCHIE

Yes, pretty young thing. She seemed to be waiting for someone. Looks like an actress, and at this time of day probably a professional. That might mean there's a company rehearsing there. Hope so.

A sound at the door. Only the sound of a dog sniffing the air. There he was. The milky eyes looking up at me. Time for our walk. Time with Old Bill.

BROOKLYN

I realised I didn't know the dog's name. I was cross with Beth. Did she really have to tell me about murderers on my first day of my new job? "Silly bitch," I said under my breath, and regretted it straightaway. Beth seemed to be a very nice woman, and she was only being concerned for a girl young enough to be her daughter.

I looked at my watch: 9.45. Still no one here. Bored now. *Booorrred!*

I tried the door again only this time with more force, and nearly fell headlong into the lobby when the door just opened. "Fuc—" I nearly swore in surprise. Must stop doing that. Living in London you hear it a lot and it's easy to catch the habit.

The lobby had that smell you always get in village halls. Carpets. Cleaning fluid. Old wood. And quiet.

Feeling like I was trespassing, I crossed the lobby and into the main hall. A decent-sized stage at one end and parquet flooring. Stacked against one wall were some tables.

Come on Brooke, I thought. *To work.* I could start by getting the room ready for the rehearsal. I went to one of the tables, turned it face-down on the floor and pulled at the trestle-type legs. They seemed to be stuck.

In my peripheral vision, a black shape loomed like a low-flying airship. I nearly screamed. Then giggled. Beth's warning about psychos in the woods had clearly got to me more than I'd thought. Beth's black dog was watching me and panting gently.

"Hello you," I said. "You scared me half to death." I gave him a friendly pat on the back and he sniffed at my face. I don't even know your name."

"That's Old Bill," said a voice, startling me again. Clearly this was the morning to be startled. An old guy stood at the door. White hair, pale skin and piercing dark eyes. I felt a surge of panic, and then got a grip on myself. This was no psycho; just an old guy with a dog… except it was Beth's dog. Bill. Well at least I now knew his name.

"Hello," I said, "the door was open. So I… well… I came in."

The old guy said nothing. Just looked. I carried on trying to put up the table.

"Actress, are you?" he said at last.

I looked up. "Yes – well, usually yes. But this time I'm stage-managing."

"Thought so," said the old guy. He had a classic, elderly actor voice. Probably every director's dream casting for the Ghost of Hamlet's father. I could just hear him saying, "Revenge his foul and most unnatural murder."

Murder again. What had got into me? "Look," I said, "you don't know how these things work do you?"

"Of course my darling." Old Hamlet walked over, and with sprightliness not immediately obvious, he unclipped the two trestle legs and the table was suddenly up.

"Oh, thank you," I gushed, suddenly feeling about fourteen and completely out of my depth. I'd been determined to be confident and professional and was now being helped by a man old enough to be my grandfather. "I'm Brooke," I said, holding out my hand.

He gave my hand a dry, wispy shake. "Charmed."

I was still so flustered I hadn't listened properly. "Charles?"

"No, my dear. Charmed. My name's Archie."

Suddenly I realised this must be the first of the actors arriving. "Pleased to meet you Archie. Now let me guess: King Edward, right?"

Archie's dark, piercing eyes flickered confusion. I tried again.

"The Lord Mayor? Hastings?" I ventured.

"No dear," Archie said at last. "No, no. I'm not an actor. Never was. Once… well, that's a story for another time." He smiled a sort of faraway smile. "I live here," he said eventually. "Just across the path in the cottage. I watched you arrive and saw you nearly fall through the door."

"Yes," I said. "I didn't think it would be open."

"Bill and I were just off for our walk, so I thought I'd pop in and say hello," said Archie.

"That's nice," I said, lamely.

"I don't often come in here now," said Archie, his eyes piercing me again, "but you remind me of someone I knew once."

I was about to quip that that was probably the worst chat-up line I'd ever heard, but stopped myself just in time. My new Hamlet's Father friend was actually just a sweet old guy who wanted to be needed.

"Well, Archie. Thanks for your help," I said.

"The pleasure, dear lady, is all mine."

For a moment I actually thought he was going to kiss my hand. Instead, he bowed his head slightly and then looked at Old Bill, who was still waiting patiently.

"Come on then Bill," he said. "Let's do our usual circuit." Then he walked with an easy gracefulness back through the lobby and out into the sunlit day with Old Bill lumbering along behind him.

ARCHIE

"The pleasure, dear lady, is all mine." What was I thinking of? "The pleasure, dear lady, is all mine?!" Get a grip on yourself man, you're in your eighties, not eighteen, and she's young enough to be your granddaughter.

So like Sheelagh. The same dark brown hair in a bob. Sheelagh wore hers with a flower over her left ear, but apart from that it's the same. Same build. Same elfin face.

Old Bill was walking beside me now. We always do this circuit. Little by little we got into a routine, ever since Old Bill was a youngster. In those days he was just Bill. The Churchill woman ran a plant society at the Institute and used to leave Bill tied by the door. Back then I would tend my vegetable garden in the mornings and stop for a cuppa at about eleven. Used to sit by the door and watch the world go by.

On this particular Wednesday the Churchill woman was late for her meeting; arriving all flustered with a box of pansies or some such. I heard her swear and saw her trying to make up her mind whether or not to run home and get something she'd forgotten.

"I'll keep an eye on Fido if you need to run back," I'd said.

She laughed and told me the dog's name was Bill. Bill and I became friends that day. The Churchill woman went back to her house, and I gave Bill some of my tea in a saucer. He lapped it up quickly and then looked up as if to say "Where's the rest?" It was a shared moment. Chaps together, against the women. Long time ago now. I'd been… what? Seventy-something I think. Bill's puppy-like eagerness had long since become a plod.

"Time for our halfway stop Bill," I said. Funny how you get into a habit. The circuit was always the same: through the back of my garden, into the woods and along the path for a couple of miles before joining a gravel track leading to Sea Lion Street and back to my house. I would always pat Bill goodbye on the green leading onto Claxton Parade and he'd scamper, or now plod, home to the Churchill woman. But here, in the woods, we'd stop. Or at least I would. Bill didn't seem to need a rest, even though in dog years he'd be older than me. I'm not as fit as I was.

I sat down on the trunk of a tree felled long ago but now forgotten. Bill sat on the ground and waited stoically. I like it here. Quiet. Birdsong. Old Bill gently panting, breath steaming in the crisp air. The crime scene tapes and that funny white tent thing are gone now. They'd been just off the path where Bill and I walk. We still came, most days. They say you're getting old when policemen look young. These chaps looked about twelve. Still, they seemed to know what they were doing. Some in those white hooded boiler suits. Other police keeping rubberneckers away. They didn't bother me so I didn't bother them.

OLD BILL

He had liked the Warm Drink Man straightaway. Before the day of the first warm drink, Bill had thought of him as the Pointy-eyed Man. Eyes bright and sharp. Then in the noises that the humans take turns in making – somehow Bill knew this was something to do with share-thinkings – Bill had heard his name. His real name. Fido.

Just once. Then the Warm Drink Man had put a dish on the ground with some warm, dark liquid and made a share-thinking noise that sounded like "Cupovtee", and Bill (Fido) had drunk it.

Everyone else called him Bill. Or now, Old Bill. He'd got used to it, even though the name didn't quite fit. A bit like a collar that was too loose. He would always think of himself as Fido. The name he'd always known.

How had the Warm Drink Man known?

The Floppy Clothes Lady didn't know. But she was nice. When he was smaller she'd made the share-thinking noises a lot when looking at him. He kept hearing "Bill" and knew she was share-thinking at him. Fido knew the Floppy Clothes Lady was nice. He just had to get used to 'Bill'.

But the Warm Drink Man had known. The Warm Drink Man with his daily dishes of dark liquid 'cupovtee' that made you feel both soft and awake at the same time.

Only the Warm Drink Man had known his true name without ever having met him before. Fido would remember him always.

BROOKLYN

"OK, start again and tell me the truth," said Scott with a knowing chuckle.

I was back in my digs at Beth's. I'd picked away at tasteless microwaved beef cannelloni and some boiled broccoli which I'd cooked in the kitchen. Thankfully Beth had been in her lounge watching television so I was spared the annoyance of having to make conversation when I least felt like it.

Now I was in my room with Scott, or at least his disembodied voice from my iPhone.

"So, how was your first day?" he asked.

"Yeah… it was OK. Met the actors, we did a read-through, or rather they did. The MD played some of the songs. We start properly tomorrow."

Scott said nothing.

Then I said, "Alright I suppose," trying to disguise a tremor in my voice. "The guy playing Richard seems a bit up himself; hardly even looked at me, let alone spoke to me. The director's an older guy. But not like favourite uncle old; more like 'sergeant major do what you're told or I'll put you on a charge' old."

Scott laughed.

"The others are OK I suppose," I added unconvincingly. Some actress I am. Can't even pretend I've had a good day and convince anyone. Even as I had the thought, I knew how wrong I was. Acting, real acting, is about truth. Not deceit. I was never going to deceive Scott because a) I didn't want to, b) he knew me better than anyone, sometimes better than I knew myself, and c) I knew that I was talking nonsense because I was feeling vulnerable.

Scott and I talked for about twenty minutes before signing off as we usually did:

ME: "Love you, Blondie."

SCOTT: "Love you, Brooklyn."

BOTH TOGETHER: "Downtown!"

Yeah, alright, I know. Cute. Or 'pass the sick bag', depending on your point of view. The punchline came from a photograph of my parents on their trip to New York. They'd done the full tourist thing: all the sights from Central Park to the Statue of Liberty. They'd even taken pictures on the subway. In the photo album was a shot of them standing beneath a sign that just said *Brooklyn – Downtown.* Scott had laughed the endearing high-pitched giggle he does when something really amuses him, and his giggling had infected me too. Mum and Dad looked on with expressions that said a mixture of "Aaaah, how sweet that they have so much in common" and "What have they been on, and where can we get some?"

A lighthearted picture, that for all I knew was taken on the very day that I was a twinkle in Dad's eye and a blush on Mum's cheek, had become one of those milestones in our relationship.

I felt better for speaking to Scott. I lay on the bed and smiled. Good job Scott wasn't an actor. He was very good at making me see things from a different point of view. A non-theatre point of view. He'd been in a school play when he was twelve, but unlike so many people who've done that, he didn't try to make out that he knew all about theatre when he didn't. And he didn't come out with the old question: "How do you manage to remember all those lines?" All actors get tired of answering that one.

After that morning when we'd met by the coffee machine we'd gone out for another coffee after work, me feeling like every kind of idiot for having been so obvious, and him beaming all over his face like a kid on a day out. We'd talked for about an hour when he said, as if he'd only just thought of it, "By the way, I've got a couple of tickets for the National on Saturday night. *Hamlet*. Wondered if you fancied coming with me?"

Would I fancy coming with him? Is the Pope a Catholic? "I'd love to… yes, that would be great." I tried not to gush.

"Great," he said. "I couldn't believe my luck."

"Flatterer," I quipped. He looked confused.

"No," Scott said, "I mean after you did such a good job of chatting me up this morning, I nipped out for an hour at lunchtime and managed to get a couple of returned tickets. We're on the sixth row of the stalls in the Olivier."

Then we both laughed. Again.

Hamlet had been superb. The Ghost of Hamlet's Father was very unconventional. Thin, wiry, and during his first appearance let out a kind of creaking wail. During that scene Scott's hand had found mine. At the interval we sat there not wanting to break the moment by going to the bar or buying ice cream.

At the end of the play the lights faded slowly to black after Fortinbras' line: "Go, bid the soldiers shoot", and there was a deep silence in darkness for several seconds before the lights came up. The applause and cheers must have been heard in the foyer. Breathtakingly brilliant.

Scott and I walked back along the South Bank past the Festival Hall, with me chattering and giggling like a schoolgirl and Scott just smiling and agreeing with everything I said. Finally I said something like, "Scott, this has been sooooo good. I'm really glad you like Shakespeare."

He said, "Well, to let you into a secret, I didn't think I did. I always thought it was boring."

"What, you mean at school?"

"Yes," said Scott, "we did *Macbeth* but I hated it."

"Oh I love *Macbeth*; greed, ambition, murder. It's the ultimate thriller."

"If you say so… I didn't actually read it," said Scott, laughing. "I just got hold of a copy of *York Notes* and blagged it."

Then we laughed again.

"This was great though. I loved it," said Scott seriously. "I even understood it. And you know, I think *Hamlet* probably counts as a thriller too."

Soul mates.

***

I lay on the bed in the blank silence of the few minutes after the phone call and gave a wan smile to Mr Tibbs in his rocking chair. At least his furry teddy bear face was friendly.

This morning, after that old guy, Archie, had gone out with Beth's dog following, the actors had started to arrive. Over-bright hellos, anecdotes of mutual acquaintances, and boring recaps of journeys from London to Dorset were the order of the day. I had that feeling you get when you go to a friend's party and don't know anybody there; when you don't quite know how to start a conversation. Except here I didn't have a drink to clutch, and to sip when conversation sagged.

Drink. Tea and coffee. Shit. I hadn't thought to bring some supplies.

When Duncan had told me about the job over a drink in a pub in Beak Street he'd said, "Jimmy can be a bit officious but you'll get on alright with him if you show initiative. He likes to start each day with a strong cup of builders' tea, and he'll expect you to make it."

I'd bridled a bit at that. Duncan laughed. "Yes, I know, it's not right, but Jimmy's very old-school and not always in a good way. You're young, you're female; you're just starting out. When he says 'Jump' he expects you to ask 'How high?'"

"I hate him already," I said.

"He's OK once you know him," said Duncan. "I'm not saying he's easy to work with and that his awkwardness is a front, because he's not, and it isn't. Especially if you're young." Duncan took a thoughtful pull at his pint. "But he has turned that theatre around. It used to be just a receiving house for tribute bands and touring variety acts. Now it has a summer rep season running ten plays over a four-month season. You don't get that unless you upset a few people along the way."

My interview with Jimmy Knowles had been during a break in auditions at Toynbee Hall. Barely ten days ago. He sat there with his long fingers steepled under his chin, steely grey eyes summing me up.

"Yes… you'll do," he said abruptly in a dry, reedy voice. "Young Duncan seems to like you, so if he's taught you what I taught him you'll fit the bill."

'Young Duncan' was nearly old enough to be my father, but his chubby, boyish face belied his forty-two years. "Don't worry Brooke," he'd said, draining his pint, "just take him with a pinch of salt, expect the occasional bawling out, and don't piss him off. You'll be fine, and it's a good theatre to get a foot in the door."

I like Duncan. Besides teaching stage management at my school he also works out there in the real world. I'd met him for a drink after his regular stint on a follow spot for *Phantom*.

Now here I was on day one of working for the infamous Jimmy Knowles, and about to fall at the first hurdle. Too late. A slam of a car door outside.

Jimmy arrived in the hall like a hurricane. "Right then, are we set up?" he asked no one in particular. No one answered.

"Hello Jimmy, good to see you again," said a thirty-something actor with a resonant voice.

"Trevor… how are you?" said Jimmy vaguely, looking around. "Well, stage manager, are we set up?" he said again, his eyes finding mine.

Take him with a pinch of salt.

"Sorry, not yet, I was about to make some tea."

Don't piss him off. And why did you apologise? Great start, Brooke.

"Ah, good idea," said Jimmy, "that's what I like; stage-management with initiative." He smiled a somewhat dry smile. "Hope you've brought some Hob-Nobs."

"Er, no, not yet." The smile vanished. "I'm going to pop to the shop across the road once I've asked what everyone likes."

"Good girl." The smile came back. My improvised recovery had worked.

"So," I said, taking charge, "who wants coffee, who wants tea – Rooibos? Fruit infusions? And do we have any advance on Hob-Nobs?"

Fifteen minutes later I was back from Bateman's with a selection of tea, coffee, skimmed milk and enough biscuits to pave a driveway.

By this time Jimmy had started work. The actors were sat around in a vague circle on the village hall's plastic chairs. Jimmy sat behind the table that Archie had helped me to put up, and the pre-read-through discussion had begun.

Eventually, feeling more like a schoolgirl on a work placement than a graduate from one of the country's top drama schools, I appeared with a tray, balancing eight mugs of steaming drinks and a selection of biscuits. Jimmy broke off from his sermon to his actors.

"Ah, capital, the tea lady's here. Thank you... er... yes, just put it down here will you? Everyone, this is our stage manager – sorry, what was your name again?"

"Brooke."

"Yes, of course you are. Brooke. Brooke Bond the tea lady. If ever I forget your name again, I'll just call you Pussy instead. That's what I do with everyone else."

A couple of the other actors laughed politely.

"You see?" said Jimmy. "They know. Especially Pussy Groat over there."

A solid-looking bearded actor bit into a fig roll and rolled his eyes as crumbs fell down his front.

Take him with a pinch of salt.

I smiled weakly. *Pussy*. He'd better not. It made me sound like something between a whore and a character from *Pulp Fiction*.

Jimmy took a sip of tea. "Nice tea though Puss – er, Brooksy. We'll have this now; then we'll have a look at the set model. You have that, don't you?"

"Set model?" I asked.

"Oh buggeration, you haven't," said Jimmy. "I suppose you haven't any tape for the mark-up either.

"Er, no," I stammered.

"Right," said Jimmy, leaving a thick silence. "Not your fault. I'll give Derek a rap over the knuckles for not telling you. You were supposed to pick up the set model from the theatre first thing and then arrive here for about twelve. I was glad you were so early, but I wondered why." He paused. "Go on, off you go. Don't need you for a bit. You don't drive, do you?"

"Er no, I'm learning but—"

"That's no good to me. Get the bus from up the road. One at quarter past the hour from Cranton Oh to the Seafront. Give Derek my compliments; tell him he's a pain in the arse and he owes both of us a drink; and don't even think about coming back here until you've got the set model, some tape for the mark-up and a supply of pencils for these useless clowns. Savvy?"

"Er, yes, OK."

"Go on then, bugger off," said Jimmy, turning back to his actors, most of whom looked at me sympathetically, apart from Trevor. He of the resonant voice and cheery "Hello Jimmy, good to see you." He seemed deep in serious thought over his script.

***

When you're used to London, public transport in the rest of the country seems painfully slow. One bus every hour from Cranton Oh to Port St Catherine Seafront. If you miss it you can just about walk the six miles instead of waiting for the next one.

The Edwardian Palace Theatre was an intoxicating place. After peering through the glass doors to the foyer and seeing no sign of life, I walked around to the stage door and pressed the intercom buzzer. A few minutes later I met Derek, the Company SM.

"Hi, I'm Brooke McCarthy."

Derek looked at me strangely for a few seconds. It was a bit like the look people gave me outside Tesco's when I'd been trying to interest them in cavity wall insulation. Vagueness mixed with uncertainty. I was about to explain who I was.

"You took your time; I was expecting you for ten."

"Yes, I'm sorry." *Why am I apologising again?*

"What was it – traffic, tube delays or forgot to set your alarm?"

"No, none of those." *Sod this. Is today National Grumpy Day?* "Actually I didn't know I had to come here first, so I went to the Institute. Then Jimmy sent me here to get the set model."

"Did he now? Right. Come with me."

We walked along a corridor past dressing room doors and *Silence* notices, then through a fire door to the scene dock, upstage left. From here I had my first real glimpse of the auditorium.

"It's beautiful," I said, pausing.

"You've not been here before?" asked Derek. I detected a Midlands twang to his accent.

"No, never. I love it." Then, not wanting risk Derek's wrath, "OK if I have a quick look?"

It's part of the etiquette of the theatre that you ask the stage manager before you go on stage when a performance isn't on. The worst that could happen is, of course, someone dropping something on you from above. Derek seemed just the type to yell, "Get off the fucking stage!"

"Yes, love, help yourself," he said. I smiled a 'thanks' and walked slowly downstage.

The house lights were on and the auditorium looked magical. Red plush velvet seats; ornate plasterwork on the edge of the circle: cherubs holding lamps in the shape of flaming torches. From downstage centre the command of the auditorium was everything you could wish for. Intimacy with over three hundred. The faint dusty smell of old fabric and paint. The regal glow of the lights. I would love to play here. Hopefully, if I could get through *Richard III*, I might.

"You're an actress then," said Derek. It was a statement. Not a question.

"Yes. Well, I'm running the show on *Richard III*, but yes I'm an actor."

"Thought so. Its only actors that want to go on stage and look out front. Crew ain't bothered. Let's go to my office."

I wasn't sure what to make of Derek. He was about forty, wore thick-lensed Woody Allen style glasses that made his eyes seem bigger, had a New York Yankees baseball hat sat far back on his head, wispy ginger hair and was dressed, as stage crew usually are, completely in black.

Derek sat behind a desk that had probably been new long before I was born, and leant back in a tatty swivel chair. I sat opposite just to the side. Derek stared at me again.

"So Brooke… Why did you come here?" That vagueness again.

"Like I said. The set model."

"Yes I know that. But why here? Why the Eddy Palace? Why Cranton Oh?" The watchful, enlarged eyes were beginning to freak me out.

"Well, I graduated about eighteen months ago, and it's been pretty quiet. I'd heard of The Palace and when one of my tutors told me there was a job here, I jumped at the chance, even if it wasn't for an acting job."

Derek nodded noncommittally. "So you've stage-managed before?"

This was feeling like I was being interviewed all over again. "Yes, in fact it was my stage management tutor who told me about this place."

"Who's that?"

"Duncan Ward."

At last a smile from Derek. "Duncan! Hell of a good bloke. He was in a pantomime here. Must be ten years."

Duncan in a pantomime! But then, why not? "Really?" I said. "Which part?"

"Dunno… I think he was one of the brokers' men or something. Like I say, long time ago. Anyway, here you go; one set model." Derek reached up to one of the shelves and pulled down a shoebox-sized model. "There's not much to it, but His Lordship wants a model, so here it is."

Derek was right. A rectangular, raised acting area. A throne upstage centre. A banner with a boar's head behind it, and either side, two pairs of cardboard pillars, midstage and upstage, which swept up overhead and made two cathedral-like arches over the action.

"The whole thing should pack down in about an hour provided everyone pulls their weight," said Derek. "If you've got prima donnas it'll take all night."

"Great," I said. "Jimmy also said I had to bring some tape for the mark-up."

"He would," said Derek. "By the way, didn't he tell you to come here first?"

"No, I just had my contract through from a lady called Gemma saying rehearsals start today at ten in Cranton Overleigh. So that's where I went."

"Bloody typical. He wants to try delegating once in a while. That way the monkeys would have an idea of what the organ grinder was up to. I'm Company Stage Manager of this place and he only saw fit to tell me he'd hired you two days ago, and then said you'd be here at ten. Doesn't seem to know the rest of us don't read minds. Never even thinks I might have an opinion on who should be working for me."

The realisation hit me. Derek would, in effect, be my boss. The presence and reputation of Jimmy Knowles filled this place. It was Jimmy who had interviewed me; Jimmy who had given me the job. It was clear that Derek hadn't even been consulted. In fairness to him, I began to see where his grumpiness might come from. Derek would be the one I would report to. It would be good if I could at least get on with him.

"So Derek, you'll be touring with us then?"

"No. I've got enough on my plate here," Derek growled. "You're on your own with this show. Just make sure the actors help you with the get-in and the strike. That's something else the colonel didn't tell me. You're under twenty-five, aren't you?"

"Yes," I said.

"Then the insurance on the tour van would be horrendous. Groaty's going to do the driving."

I didn't think it would be wise to tell Derek I didn't yet drive at all. "Groaty?"

"Keith Groat. Big bloke. Beard. Works here a lot. You'll meet him."

I remembered the solid-looking actor spilling fig roll crumbs down his front. "Right, thanks," I said. "I guess I should be getting back."

"I would if I were you. Nothing else His Majesty needed?"

I thought for a moment and then decided it might be wiser not to pass on Jimmy's message. "No, that's it. I'll see you anon."

"Not if I see you first."

That seemed a strange reply, so I said nothing and went. *Not if I see you first?*

I was halfway back to the bus stop before I remembered Jimmy's request to bring a supply of pencils for 'these useless clowns'. I didn't fancy going back to the theatre and Derek. Surely all actors bring a pencil to rehearsals?

Expect the occasional bawling out, and don't piss him off.

I spent a couple of quid in The Works, and bought an enormous pack of HBs with eraser tips. Better not upset the boss on the first day.

***

I arrived back at the Institute, glanced into the garden of the cottage and looked at the windows, hoping to catch a glimpse of the old guy from this morning. Not a sign of him. The windows looked dusty, with peeling paint on the frames. The garden was overgrown.

I went into the village hall and took a seat at the side. The read-through was clearly over and Jimmy was telling the actors his view of the play.

"So the Queen Margaret scene is crucial to this production. Queen Margaret's curses on Hastings, Rivers, Richard himself… Buckingham.

"*O, but remember this another day,*

When he shall split thy very heart with sorrow,

And say poor Margaret was a prophetess… All come to pass in the course of the play."

Jimmy turned to me. "Ah, there you are Brooksy. You're bang on cue. Always a good sign when stage management are on time. Let's have a look at the set model. Come on, don't be shy, this lot don't bite. I do, but I won't today."

I set up the model on Jimmy's table, and the others wandered over.

Jimmy carried on: "Gather round ladies and gentlemen, have a look at this. As I was saying, the prophecies all come true; so on Buckingham's death we'll do clever things with projection onto this screen here..." Jimmy pointed at the back of the set model to where there was a gauze banner with a boar's head painted on it "...and we'll see Eleanor's scary face as Queen M as she says:

"*O, but remember this another day.*"

Eleanor smiled ruefully at Jimmy and there was a general mutter of assent that this was a good idea.

"Anyway, that's the thinking, do you see? The memories of Margaret's curses, together with the murders he's committed and the wrongs he's done, all come back to haunt Richard the night before Bosworth:

"*The lights burn blue. It is now dead midnight.*

Cold fearful drops stand on my trembling flesh.

What do I fear? Myself? There's none else by... and so on. There'll be a lot of tech to sort out in that scene... anything else this lot need to know, Brooksy?" Jimmy looked at me again.

Anything else? I don't know, I've only just been given the stupid model. I knew no more about it than any of them.

"Er, no, not really," I said, trying to sound like I knew what I was talking about, then suddenly remembered Derek's words about everybody helping with the set-build and strike. "Actually yes," I said, gaining confidence as I spoke, "the whole thing should take a couple of hours to unpack and put up," (I was guessing that bit) "and just about an hour to pack down provided everyone helps."

There was a rather damp silence with all eyes on me. Especially Jimmy's. I went on: "I just want to say at this stage that I'll need some help with the get-in and the strike," I added lamely, feeling myself reddening.

"Well then," said Jimmy, "consider yourselves told. That's it. We'll stop here for lunch."

Keith Groat came over to me. "Well said. I'm Keith by the way." He shook me by the hand. "Rivers, and van monkey. I've done a few tours like this. They're great as long as everyone mucks in. Pain in the arse when they don't. You don't drive then?"

"No, not yet."

"Useful if you want to stage-manage."

"I don't," I said. "I mean, well, I'm stage-managing this, but I'm an actor really."

I walked over to Bateman's with Keith and bought some sandwiches for lunch. Jimmy went to the pub with John Murray, and by the time we came back the others were sitting down with lunch boxes, flasks and newspapers.

Apart from Keith Groat, who seemed a very bluff, no-nonsense type, the others were Eleanor Boscombe playing Queen Margaret, Rachel Powell as Lady Anne, John Murray as Hastings, Trevor George as Buckingham, Finlay Beckett, who didn't seem to be much older than me, as a general actor-musician who would play a variety of instruments during the play and would also play Lord Stanley, Clarence and various other roles, and Trevor Knightsbridge as Richard.

Conversation was a bit sparse. Fairly normal for a first day I guess, so after a while I pulled out my copy of the script and idly flicked through a few pages. I found myself looking at Act One Scene Three:

O, but remember this another day,
When he shall split thy very heart with sorrow…

I quite liked Jimmy's idea: the misdeeds of Richard's past returning to haunt him. I looked up. Trevor Knightsbridge was watching me carefully from across the room. Our eyes met, and then he glanced away, like people do when you catch their eye when they are seated opposite you on a tube train. Something about his glance made me uncomfortable. I went back to my script and Queen Margaret's earlier speech.

. . . take heed of yonder dog!
Have not to do with him, beware of him.
Sin, death, and hell have set their marks on him.

I looked up. Trevor Knightsbridge was no longer there.

ARCHIE

Another thing about getting older: time shrinks.

Things that happened, say fifty years ago seem more recent. The Coronation. Bringing Sheelagh to see where I'd grown up. Fifty years? Sixty? That rhododendron bush I like to look at in the mornings. Ten years. Must be. The actors now in the hall with the nice young girl. *The pleasure, dear lady, is all mine.* That was definitely yesterday.

No breakfast again this morning. Probably an old man thing. Don't seem to sleep much either.

This morning I would go over to the hall. Hopefully see Brooke again. I fished in the kitchen table drawer and pulled out the key I'd always had. When I'd sold the hall after Sheelagh died and it ended up in the hands of the Philistines, no one had thought to change the locks. Typical village hall committee. Everyone thought that someone else would do it, and so young Martin Helgin was in charge of security in a hall with keys that he knew nothing about.

Including mine.

It was early. Not long after dawn. That's the other thing about getting old. When you don't sleep much, five o'clock, six, seven, don't seem to matter much. Early. That was all. The birds were singing. It was just getting light.

I walked into the empty hall full of my memories. In some ways it now more closely resembled the schoolroom I'd known as a boy. Before the best memories. The memories to do with Sheelagh, and her inspiration to turn it into a theatre.

I stood at the end of the hall where the stage had been, and to where, long ago, the teacher had stood on a raised platform facing pupils on wooden benches.

"Archibald Stephens, come up here." I could still hear Miss Beck's severe voice, and could see my nine-year-old self rise nervously from my seat halfway back. Miss Beck had given me a large book of Shakespeare, open at the start of *Richard III*.

"Now then, Master Stephens, you're going to read the first speech to the class," she'd said, in a voice that brooked no contradiction. "Loud and clear now."

Behind me on the blackboard the speech was written out for the rest of the class to follow.

"And then we're all going to learn this speech off by heart."

I could sense my classmates' reluctance.

"For its poetry, its language, and then we're going to learn about this period of history. The House of York. The House of Lancaster."

I could still remember it. Felt like only ten years ago… actually it was more like seventy.

"*Now is the winter of our discontent*
Made glorious summer by this sun of York…"

The faces of the other children; all glad I had been picked instead of them.

Between those far-off schoolroom days and now, this room had become a successful theatre – The Hideaway. Now, years later, a play was rehearsing here which I'd been made to read from as a schoolboy in this very room.

Meant to be.

I looked idly round. The table I'd helped young Brooke (*Sheelagh*) to put up was still there. A set model, a builders' tape measure and some rolls of tape left from the day before.

Tape. Back in the days of The Hideaway we'd used chalk for marking the position of as yet unbuilt scenery.

I felt a surge of nostalgia. That's an old man thing too. You realise over time that there is less time left than you've already had, and you remember fondly. Almost before I knew I was doing it, I was studying the set model, taking measurements. I was working in the theatre for the first time since Sheelagh died, ripping the tape off the spool and sticking it to the floor. Position of the big banner screen, upstage centre. The pillars either side supporting an archway. Throne. No, don't just mark the position Archie, what do we have in the scene dock?

The van from the Edwardian Palace had come during the late afternoon bringing a selection of costumes and props and bits of scenery to be used for the show.

A throne. It looked familiar. It came from here in the first place and had been taken to the Edwardian Palace with everything else when The Hideaway closed. In fact I'm pretty sure that I helped make it. Many years ago. Now it was back in its proper place. Where it was built. By me. Used several times, and painted many times in accordance with the play. Gold with garish painted jewels for King Crumble in *Jack and the Beanstalk*. A dark pewter colour for *Macbeth*. Dulled with dust. Chipped and showing specks of bright gold beneath. But sturdy enough.

It would do.

Better get it in position before Sheelagh gets here.

BROOKLYN

"Right then stage manager, are we set up?"

"No Jimmy of course we're not, we've only just come in. Give me a break."

"Don't give me any bloody lip, or I'll call the police. I need to get working on the show sometime before murder. Come on girl. Still looking, get with it, and while you're at it make some Hob-Nobs. Lynn Arthur drive some tea, get the bus to Cranton Overleigh near Port St Catherine Seafront with only one bus an hour; consider yourself told."

Devastated parents are appealing… pathway where council cuts mean the path through the woods is no longer illuminated at night—

"Appalling inefficiency. Are we set up… are we set up? Set up?"

Information leading—

"No Jimmy I've told you, we've only just come in the woods, give me a fatal fracture to the skull."

"Right then stage manager, are we set up?"

"Yes we are, all set."

"Set up the *Today* programme on Radio 4 with John Humphrys and Mishal Husain."

"It's… set up."

"Ten past eight."

Up… up.

I woke with a start.

My iPhone alarm had sounded at half past seven. I'd blearily reached out and switched on my radio, meaning to listen for a few minutes while I came to, and then I would get up.

I had just drifted off to sleep again.

My dream had been a surreal mix of whatever had been on the news and Jimmy. I didn't like to admit it, but I guess I was scared of him. His personality was huge. He clearly didn't take any crap, and he didn't seem to care if people liked him or not. Jimmy know-it-all Knowles. My way or the highway.

But his ideas were good. The Edwardian Palace was a good theatre, because of him. I just had to try and get on with him.

"Right then, are we set up?" His first words yesterday morning had clearly been directed at me. Anyone with half a brain cell walking into an empty hall, with only a table in place and a few chairs, would know straightaway that nothing was set up. It had really irritated me, and I'd only escaped a telling-off by a quick recovery concerning tea and coffee. Which I'd very nearly forgotten altogether.

I threw back the covers and did my usual morning routine. Quick shower, dressed, check for messages.

Scott.

Hope you slept well gorgeous. Have a good day ☺

PS: Don't let the luvvies grind you down.

Luvvies. Actors don't call themselves that, any more than they describe being out of work as 'resting'.

I smiled.

My phone beeped again. Scott.

PS. I love you a whole bunch of bananas.

Something about that unusual way of saying 'I love you' nearly made me cry.

I texted back: *Love you too… as much as pips in a pomegranate.*

A reply came straight back: *Take care of yourself and don't walk through the woods.* No humour in that. Scott in serious mode.

Missing me. Bless him. The plea to be careful an expression of his love for me.

God, I'm thinking like a schoolgirl.

I quickly brushed my hair and went down to breakfast. What was so bad about the woods anyway? Oh yeah. The murder the other week. The girl on the front of people's newspapers on the tube. Whatever.

Old Bill wagged his tail and plodded over to where I sat myself down for my breakfast. *Right. Let's get today off to a good start.* Forget Shreddies. Today it would be muesli with some yogurt and toast.

Beth Churchill appeared from the living room. "Morning Brooke, all set for day two?"

"Yes, I guess so. The first day's always the hardest. Lots of nervous energy."

"The thing I can never understand is how you manage to remember all those lines."

That one again. I came out with the usual answer that actors give. It's practice. The memory is like a muscle. The more you exercise it, the stronger it gets.

Old Bill gave a whimper and pawed my leg.

"Morning Bill, I'm sorry, have you missed me?" I said. Hazy doggy eyes looked up at me. He pawed at me again as if he wanted to shake my hand. I took his paw in mine and gently shook it, as if I were a salesman greeting a client. "Hello Mr Bill, how are you?"

Bill looked dolefully up at me and then sniffed my hand. Stretched up towards my face and sniffed again.

"Oh sorry Bill," I said, "I'm not wearing my Chanel today: that's for the only other man in my life and he doesn't have fur and a tail."

Beth chuckled like an indulgent grandparent whose grandchild is being given attention by a stranger.

Old Bill continued his sniffing. Then sat back and looked at me, head cocked to one side, and with a sound somewhere between a whimper and a trill, gave a gentle lick to my hand and then nuzzled into me for some more attention.

"Well," said Beth, "I'm not sure what you've done to deserve all that, but you've clearly got a fan."

I laughed and continued my small talk with Beth. Acting, the theatre and Scott. No, he wasn't an actor as well. Works in the city. Yes, he's got a proper job. No, I haven't been on TV. Yes, I'd like to, but it hasn't happened yet. Yes, I'll remember you when I'm famous. All the usual stuff.

OLD BILL

The walks with the Warm Drink Man were always nice. Since the Bad Thing happened, Old Bill never wanted the Warm Drink Man to go on his own.

Through the woods.

A long time ago, when Bill could run, not plod, he caught a bobber. Long ears. Fluffy tail. Brown fur. Didn't know why he did it. Just did. Chased. Bit. Shook. The Bobber stopped.

Still.

He had smelt it on himself. The Cain Scent. Didn't like it. It faded after a day. On creatures it always fades after a day. On men it never fades. The Cain Scent on men gives creatures the fear and dread of them.

In the woods Bill saw someone with the Cain Scent. They saw him. Made share-thinking noises at him, but hadn't stopped.

Then the people with the white tents had arrived where the Bad Thing had happened. Bill didn't know what the Bad Thing was, but it had to do with the Cain Scent.

Mustn't let the Warm Drink Man go there alone. Would go and see him today.

The Floppy Clothes Lady never went to the Warm Drink Man's place. But the Young One did.

Must take care of the Young One. Here she is. She starts share-thinking with the Floppy Clothes Lady. Bill hears his name and other share-thinking noise. The Young One smiles. More share-thinking. He hears his name again. Bill, and a word that sounds like "Sha-nell". He tests her for scent. Nice, warm, Young One scent. Needs to tell her. He tries a share-thinking noise. She makes a happy share-thinking and smiles, but doesn't understand. Bill kisses her hand.

Old Bill saw a lot of people around the building near where the Warm Drink Man lives. He went back there later in the day after his walk. He likes to go there, but this time he stayed and watched because one of the people troubled him. Bad person.

The someone with the Cain Scent.

BROOKLYN

I came pounding down the stairs at twenty past nine feeling quite annoyed with myself. Although I'd had plenty of time, I was now in danger of being late. Crazy. The so-called Institute was only ten minutes' walk down the road. That's why it's so easy to be late. It's so near that you leave it till the last minute. With rehearsals at ten, I would need at least thirty minutes to do a quick mark-up and set out some furniture.

Sod it, I would take the shortcut through the woods, and just not tell Beth.

Or Scott.

As I walked down the path to the road, suddenly there was Old Bill next to me. He looked up at me doggily, and then walked beside me. "Hello Bill," I said, "I haven't got time for you now," and then calling to Beth: "Beth! Bill's out the front here, is that OK?"

Beth appeared from around the side of the house. "Yes, he does that. I let him out after breakfast and he takes himself for a walk. Saves me the bother. Don't worry, he'll be fine."

Bill and I walked along more slowly than I wanted. I crossed the Green to the road, and then over to the cycleway and footpath through the woods, which I knew would cut several hundred yards off my journey. Suddenly Bill crossed in front of me and I all but tripped right over him.

"Easy there fella," I said. Bill was standing right in front of me. I tried to get by. He was still in my way. "Come on Old Bill, I've got to get to work."

Bill gave a kind of growling, yelping bark. A bit like in the live action version of *101 Dalmatians* when the dogs meet Cruella de Vil. I was a bit taken aback, and slightly scared. *Really?* I hadn't planned on telling Scott or Beth that I'd gone through the dreaded woods to the hall, but I didn't think I needed to worry about an old black Labrador. OK. Whatever. I would go the street way.

Feeling like a kid again, I marched along Sea Lion Street to the hall, with Bill plodding along behind me, probably to make sure I didn't go back. I was flustered and annoyed with myself. Had I in all seriousness not taken a perfectly acceptable route to work because a dog had told me not to? Must be out of my mind. I was out of sorts. And nearly late.

Shit. Jimmy was here already. A dark green Ford Focus was on the path between the old guy's cottage and the hall. I'd really wanted to be there ahead of everyone else today. I needed to get the hall ready. With any luck Jimmy might have met the old guy and be talking to him.

Archie's cottage looked blank. The door open by an inch. I very nearly gave it a push and shouted hello. No time today. Bill stopped by the porch and waited for Archie to come out.

"See you later Bill, have a nice day."

I went into the Institute, trying my best to look efficient, cool and ready for a day's work.

Jimmy was already seated in a chair behind the table with the set model in front of him, studying the script. He scarcely looked up as I came in.

"Ah, there you are stage manager, are we set up?" Already, on day two, I was learning to hate that phrase.

"No, not yet…" I started to say. Then I noticed. Jimmy must have already been here for over half an hour. Masking tape in perfectly straight lines was stuck to the floor where the set would be. Positions of the two downstage exits clearly marked in. Clearly the work of someone who knew exactly how to do a floor mark-up.

The benches were in position for the top of the show, and backstage centre was the throne which had come up in the van from the theatre late yesterday afternoon before we finished for the day.

Jimmy had said, "That's it ladies and gentlemen, we'll stop there. Brooksy, organise this rabble and get the van offloaded will you?"

And so, feeling like a schoolgirl organising a staff meeting, I'd said something along the lines of "OK everyone, this is where the fun really starts. Perhaps we could form a work chain and pass everything from one person to another."

We'd all drifted outside to where Derek had parked the van next to the hall and an assortment of furniture and costumes had taken about ten minutes to offload. After that, I'd left at about the same time as everyone else, everyone except for Jimmy, Derek and Keith. First thing the next morning, I would set everything up for the day.

Except I was late. No, actually I wasn't. It was still thirty minutes before the rehearsal. But the boss was here before I was. That meant I was late. And now the boss had done the job he was paying me for. Not good. His "Ah, there you are stage manager, are we set up?" was clearly a sarcastic reproof.

"I'm sorry Jimmy, I meant to get here before this." *Apologising again, must try and stop that.*

Jimmy didn't look up.

I tried again; "Well, I'll get the kettle on. Builders' tea again?"

No reply.

"Jimmy?"

Finally he looked up from his script. No smile. "Yes, thank you Brooksy… and by the way, when we're at work, it's Mr Knowles." He looked down again.

I felt myself blush. " Right… OK. No problem". Another loud silence. "I'll umm… get the kettle on then."

Another great start Brooke. Get here late, your boss does your job for you and then makes you address him formally when clearly everybody else calls him Jimmy. "Hello Jimmy, good to see you."

I remembered Duncan's words: "Jimmy's very old-school and not always in a good way."

Although I'm new to all this, most people in the industry now seem to use first names. So frequently, that when you meet someone from The Old School it takes you by surprise. And it gets embarrassing.

I filled the silence that had descended like a safety curtain between Mr Knowles and me by making the drinks in the kitchen, and by the time I'd finished, the others had arrived.

Rachel Powell came over to me. "Morning Brooke." She smiled. "Got over your first day?"

"Yes, I guess so," I said, squeezing the tea bag that I'd left marinating in Mr Knowles' cup of tea, and trying to sound cheerful.

"Your first job out of school?" asked Rachel.

"Yes, first proper theatre job." The truth was that I'd already played Nina in *The Seagull* for a short profit-share run. We'd played for five nights in The Space and had only just broken even. I'd been out of college a matter of weeks; the rest of the cast were my former classmates. It was exciting, and fun. And unpaid. Not proper.

We'd invited agents. One or two of whom actually came, and one of them signed me. So it had all been worth doing.

But now, some eighteen months into the real world, *The Seagull* seemed like a kind of last hurrah from college. Which is kind of what it had been.

"So what else have you been up to?" asked Rachel.

"Bits and pieces really. I had a nice corporate video a few months back, some role play; I got seen for *Holby City* but I didn't get it."

"It's good that you're getting seen though," said Rachel. "That's more than half the battle in this business."

"Do you have an agent Rachel?"

"Yes," she said. "I'm with Con Covington."

I raised my eyebrows. "Good for you," I said, trying to keep the envy out of my voice. Constance Covington Associates was one of the better-known agencies. Constance herself, or one of her lieutenants, usually went to drama school showcases, and in the past few years had cherry-picked some of the best talent and put them into really good jobs. That kind of luck was what we all aspired to. Getting picked up by one of the big agencies straight from drama school was a huge boost. And a huge fall if, within the first year or so, you hadn't earned the agency any big bucks, and they dropped you in favour of someone else.

"Actually that's kind of why I wanted to catch you before we start," said Rachel. "I spoke to Jimmy last night after everyone else had gone. I'd been putting it off to be honest, but I'm not going to be here for the rest of today, and I know he's going to ask you to fill in for me. He was pretty pissed off with me and made me feel so bad I felt like telling him where to stick it. Glad I didn't. He's alright really, just a bit scary."

"You can say that again," I said quietly. "So where are you off to today?"

"Back to London. I've got an important meeting."

"What, you mean like a casting meeting?"

"Yes. I'm afraid I can't tell you what it's for, but it's a big one. Constance has been trying to get me seen for it since before I got this job, and between you and me, said that if she has to pull me out of this job in order to do it then she will."

Rachel and I were practically whispering, like two young girls sharing confidences that the grown-ups weren't meant to hear. Rachel went on. "Constance said she'd phone the Eddy Pally office and speak to that Gemma woman, but I said I'd prefer to speak to Jimmy myself first. That didn't go down well with Con, but I'm not that well-established and quite honestly if I don't get this film job then I'm going to need this one, and if I can avoid upsetting Jimmy I will."

Film job. *I'm afraid I can't tell you what it's for, but it's a big one.* Probably a major part in one of the big blockbuster franchises. Hence the vow of secrecy. The sort of part most actors dream of. The sort of part only the top agencies ever get to hear about.

Part of me was really pleased for Rachel. Part of me ached for an opportunity like that for myself, and all of me felt glad that Rachel had chosen to confide in me. I felt like I'd made a friend.

"Dying of thirst over here," yelled Jimmy. Shit. I'd been so immersed in my talk with Rachel I'd forgotten Mr Knowles' stupid cup of stupid strong stupid tea.

Rachel looked at me and rolled her eyes. "I'll do it," she whispered, and took the large white steaming mug over to the boss.

"Here you are Jimmy; special delivery from Tetley's," she said lightly. I waited for the thunderclap. None came. Jimmy was clearly more pissed off with me than he was with Rachel. And I wasn't the one taking a day out. I hadn't even been late. All I'd done was to arrive later than he had.

Rachel came back over to me, pulling a face that jokily said 'tread carefully, he's in a mood.'

"So when are you off?" I asked.

"Any minute now. My digs are just along the Port St Catherine Road. I'm heading to the Seafront and then getting the trains up to town. I had some time, so I wanted to let you know first."

"Thank you. That's kind," I said. And I meant it. Nice of her to even think of it. Suddenly I felt better about my job, and better about the fact that I was here.

"Right then ladies and gentlemen, let's get started," commanded Jimmy. "Before we do, I have an announcement; our esteemed Miss Powell is taking herself off to London today for some meeting that I'm not even allowed know about, so Brooksy, you don't seem to be doing much at the moment except making the tea, and I even had to nag you for that, so we'll see if you're any better at filling in for Lady Anne. Just make sure you mark down all the moves. Right, go on then Rachel, bugger off, and tell your friends in Hollywood that I found you here first. Right, thank you ladies and gentlemen, we'll take it from the top and see what we've got so far. You still here Rachel? Don't forget to give Brooksy your script."

Jimmy sat back down. Rachel waved a silent goodbye at the room in general. I smiled and mouthed "Good luck" back at her.

'What we've got so far' was not actually that much by way of blocking. Yesterday after lunch there had been a lot of discussion about the concept of the play. Then Finlay, our actor-muso, played some of the theme music for the show, with Jimmy enthusing about how it would all fit.

"First positions please," said Jimmy. "Now remember, it's an after-war party. Finlay, we'll go for the martial theme and then segue into the light jazz."

The cast shuffled into position. Trevor George said, "Brooke, you're here next to me." We were mid stage left.

Finlay struck up on his guitar with something that sounded like march music, while the cast milled around doing the 'I'm at a party' type acting that Jimmy had blocked yesterday. I was holding my own script rather than Rachel's, as I'd been an efficient DSM and had marked down the moves as they'd been set.

"Yes, good, very nice, keep the hubbub going," prompted Jimmy. " Now, Finlay, into the jazz section." Finlay's nimble fingers changed rhythm into a 40s-style big band number.

"And… off you go Trevor. Brooksy, get out of his way for God's sake!"

I had been so caught up with listening to Finlay's incredible playing that I had drifted centre stage, right in front of where Trevor Knightsbridge was to begin his first speech.

"Sorry," I whispered at him as he went downstage.

"Don't keep apologising woman, we'll think you've done something wrong!" yelled Jimmy.

"Sorry," I said before I could stop myself. The rehearsal stopped with a few stifled sniggers.

"Alright, alright, not bad, that's the shape of it. Finlay: first class. Everyone else, we need silent mime during the Souza march. The lights will be low at that point. Brooksy, make a note of that. Then as soon as we're into the jazz section it's like a top government cocktail party. Chatter chatter chatter. Trevor, provided stage management don't get in your way and we actually get to your bit, remember the essence of it is 'Everyone's having a party, but I hate it.' Rrrrrrrright. Off we go again."

My cheeks were burning again. The man seemed to be deliberately trying to make me feel incompetent. This time I stayed as far stage left as I dared, and I heard Trevor Knightsbridge's opening speech properly for the first time.

Trevor had not spoken to me at all yet. In fact, I sensed he was actually avoiding looking at me. The speech was good though. Light at first, even jokey, but then becoming darker and cold towards the end with: "*I am determined to prove a villain and hate the idle pleasures of these days… plots have I laid…*"

The voice of a killer.

ARCHIE

I felt better this morning than I had in years. I'd been working in the theatre again. My theatre. The one Sheelagh and I had given birth to.

After crawling about with sticky tape and lugging that great throne across the floor I'd been exhausted, and had come back to the cottage in need of a rest. I never seemed to need breakfast these days. Just needed to sit down and wait for Sheelagh to turn up and enjoy her surprise. Sheelagh?

Brooke. That was her name. So like Sheelagh. Except no flower in her hair.

I would wait for her and then go to the hall for another chat. Before the others turned up.

Then Jimmy Knowles turned up. Got out of his dark green car humming some tune from an opera. He would be the first one to see my surprise for young Brooke.

Shortly after that Old Bill turned up for our walk. I just caught a glimpse of Brooke disappearing into the hall. I would have gone in after her if Jimmy Knowles hadn't been there. Feeling like a parent whose child has discovered the hidden Christmas presents too soon, I looked down at Bill.

"Come on then Fido. Off we go again."

He cocked his head to one side and it seemed as if the milky eyes sparkled.

We went over Act One Scene One a few times. We were all getting used to Finlay's playing. Finding out where the music fitted in, and where to be at any given point. I dutifully noted down every move that would affect Rachel when she came back.

Next was the scene with Richard, Clarence and Brackenbury; in other words Trevor Knightsbridge, Finlay Beckett and Keith Groat. For that scene, I sat down next to Mr Knowles and watched. I had to admit that Trevor was going to be extremely good. There was something very intense about him, and his speeches where Richard is delighting in his own treachery gave me chills.

I was secretly impatient to get to the next scene; the one between Richard and Lady Anne. In other words: me. Just for today. It would in effect, be my audition for Jimmy Knowles and the Edwardian Palace. My chance to show that I was really an actor.

It's a great scene too. In the play, Richard, who at this point is just the Duke of Gloucester, needs to marry Lady Anne, the daughter of the Earl of Warwick, in order to secure his path to the throne of England. The problem is that Lady Anne hates him. I mean, really *hates* him. Richard had killed her husband only three months previously, and in this scene Lady Anne is weeping over the dead body of her husband's father; also killed by Richard. Richard comes to her, and over the freshly killed body of her father-in-law, asks her to marry him, saying that it was love for her that made him kill her husband. The stuff of great drama.

And it was a scene I knew quite well. At college it had been this scene that I had worked on during my pre-finals for a Shakespeare masterclass. An actor called Alan Pinder had been 'my' Richard. Alan was small, wiry, with a firecracker energy, and the pair of us had loved the sharp dialogue and the drama played for high stakes: Richard wants to marry Anne. Anne wants Richard dead.

Trevor was coming near to the end of his speech for the third time. He was already off-book, and giving an intense, brooding performance.

"What though I killed her husband and her father?
The readiest way to make the wench amends
Is to become her husband and her father,
The which will I – not all so much for love
As for another secret close intent
By marrying her which I must reach unto.
But yet I run before my horse to market:
Clarence still breathes; Edward still lives and reigns;
When they are gone, then must I count my gains."

"Thank you Trevor. Yes, that's it," said Jimmy. "Charm us. Tell us what you're going to do, then say 'Watch me do it.' Do you see?" He looked up at Trevor over his glasses, his forehead creasing in even ripples.

"Yar, I do," replied Trevor.

I hate it when people say 'Yar.' Sounds too arty to be true.

"Charm and menace. The more you charm us, the more evil you become. A bit like Iago," said Jimmy.

Trevor gave an expression of profound agreement. Or if I was being unkind, I might say profound arse-kissing.

"Absolutely. *When devils will their blackest sins put on they do suggest at first with heavenly shows as I do now.*"

"Ex-actly," said Jimmy emphatically. He split the word in two and made a pointing gesture as he said it. "'*I can smile, and murder while I smile.*' Yes, that's it."

Trevor went on: "In fact I have a line in Act One Scene Three:

"And thus I clothe my naked villainy
With odd old ends stolen forth of Holy Writ,
And seem a saint, when most I play the devil."

"That's right, dear boy. Good… good."

I'd started to wonder how long this Shakespearean tennis game would go on for when Jimmy said, "Right then, onwards… what's next? Oh, we don't have Rachel, that's a bugger."

I was already on my feet. "It's OK, I'll read in."

"Hmm?" Jimmy looked up distractedly.

"I'll read in," I repeated. Jimmy just looked.

Trevor said, "That'd be good," in a voice that told me it wouldn't be.

"Yes," said Jimmy eventually, "we can get a sense of the shape of it. Right then, Keith and John, you're going to be my stretcher-bearers in this, and we'll have the corpse dummy on one of the benches. Brooksy, make a note to tell Derek we need some long poles for the handles."

Keith and John picked up one of the benches from backstage.

"That's it chaps," said Jimmy, "and on you come with it, and it needs to go downstage centre. Brooksy, where are you? Ah, there you are."

I'd been making the note for Derek in the script and in

those few seconds Jimmy had stepped between me and the stretcher party.

"So you're here, do you see?" said Jimmy, manhandling me to centre stage. "Get yourself – I mean Rachel – here straight after *count my gains*, and Keith and John, that's your cue. Ooooo…kaaaaay… off we go."

I found myself centre stage, script in hand for my first appearance in front of the scary Jimmy Knowles. Trevor gave the last few words of his speech. On came Keith, John and the stretcher.

"*Set down, set down your honourable load –*

If honour may be shrouded in a hearse…"

"Yes, yes, all beautifully spoken Brooksy, but boring as batshit. Those first words need to be more of a command, do you see? Let's go again."

"*Set down!*"

"No. No. No. No. No. No. No… No." There was a long pause before the very pointed final 'no' while Jimmy looked at me with exasperation. "Keith and John, take yourselves off again. Cue please Trevor. I want to see if stage management can act."

I'll bloody well show him then, I thought.

"*Set down!*" I commanded the stretcher party. Then I paused. They looked. I held the pause as long as I dared. "*Set down your honourable load – if honour may be shrouded in a hearse.*"

Keith and John put down the bench.

"*Whilst I awhile obsequiously lament*

Th'untimely fall of virtuous Lancaster."

Going well so far, he hasn't stopped me yet. Now come on Brooke, this is the dead body of your father.

"Poor key-cold figure of a holy king,
Pale ashes of the house of Lancaster,
Thou bloodless remnant of that royal blood,
Be it lawful that I invocate thy ghost..."

"Yes, Brooksy, not bad, that's the shape of it," said Jimmy dismissively, "not much point ploughing through the rest of it; we'll get the proper actress back tomorrow. Let's just go to the end of the speech. So John and Keith, pick up the bench again, make a note Brooksy, that happens around about 'come now to Chertsey'."

The proper actress. So much for my trying to impress Jimmy Knowles.

"Riiiightt-ooooh!" boomed Jimmy, "onwards. Brooksy, just top and tail the big speeches. Don't want to spend too long on this without the real actress."

"Actually Jimmy, It would be helpful for her to read the whole speeches," said Trevor. "I'm only just off book, and it'll help with what I'm doing."

"Good God man, what are you planning on doing? Juggling? Fire-eating?"

"No, I mean with the intentions."

"Alright Trevor, if all this method acting works for you, then fine. Just don't try and be a babbling brook. And Brooksy, that's a note for you too. Babbling Brooksy." Jimmy chuckled. "Oooookaaaaay... when you're ready."

And so it was that, thanks to Trevor, who I had started not to like very much, I got my chance to show Jimmy Knowles that I could act. We went through the scene once, all the way through. In the Penguin edition that's fully eight pages from the end of the speech Jimmy had interrupted. Except this time he didn't interrupt. Not once. Trevor didn't have his script in his hand at all. I had mine, but didn't look at it much. I thanked my good fortune that it was this scene I had worked so hard at while at college. The dialogue was all still there in my memory, ready to be unleashed. *However do you remember all those lines?* They become part of you. Trevor and I were two professionals working the text. Listening. Reacting. Living the characters.

Trevor was brilliant. Dark eyes filled with emotion and crying real tears: "*What these sorrows could not thence exhale, thy beauty hath, and made them blind with weeping.*" On the first time through, and with a stand-in, that was impressive.

Those eyes, now glittering with charm: "*Vouchsafe to wear this ring.*"

I could feel my voice husky with emotion: "*To take is not to give.*"

Trevor's voice practically a whisper as he caressed my hand and kissed it:

"*Look how my ring encompasseth thy finger,*
Even so thy breast encloseth my poor heart."

His hand cupped my breast. Every instinct told me to recoil. But I didn't. Because Lady Anne wouldn't. Not at this point. I just held the gaze from those unblinking coal-black eyes. Then a few lines later, we were at Lady Anne's exit line: "*Imagine I have said farewell already.*"

Trevor started the next big soliloquy: "*Was ever woman in this humour wooed?*"

"Excellent… Bravo. Well done," said Jimmy. "Didn't want to stop you, that was firing very nicely on all cylinders. Brooksy, better warn Rachel that he's going to squeeze her tit on that line. I'm sure you remember where."

"Sorry about that Brooklyn," said Trevor, incredibly still wiping away a tear, "it just seemed right."

"No it's fine. I liked it," I said.

Jimmy harrumphed and some of the others laughed.

Realising what I'd said, I then blurted out, "No, I mean I liked it in the scene… I mean it was right… It was fine." Somehow I didn't sound convincing. The truth was that my flesh had crawled, but even I wasn't sure whether that was me, Brooke, being creeped out by intense Trevor, or me, Brooke, as Lady Anne instinctively reacting to creepy Richard of Gloucester.

"Yes, anyway, better warn Dame Rachel," said Jimmy, "but bloody good Trevor. Very nice shape to the scene. And well read Brooksy. Good job. Right, onwards, then we'll stop for a quick break. Stage manager, kettle on please. OK Trevor, let's have a crack at the next big speech."

Well read? Well read! I felt a rush of indignation. I'd scarcely read any of it. Once Trevor and I had hit our stride I'd been flying with it. Felt it. The emotions; the shape of the scene. The pauses. And I'd been good. Damn good. *Well read Brooksy, now go and make the tea!* Was that really what my drama school training had led to? Making tea for some old fart who's so up himself he can't tell the difference between a rehearsal read and a performance?

"Brooke, that was a splendid job." Eleanor Boscombe had come into the kitchen where I was washing the cups. She was in her mid to late fifties, with dark hair and light grey eyes that twinkled warmly at you above the half-glasses she used when reading. "You could have heard a pin drop in there."

"Thank you Eleanor," I said, trying to quickly hide the fact that I was seething with frustration at Mr Knowles.

"It's unusual that he didn't stop you," said Eleanor. "I did Lady Bracknell for him a few years ago and he hardly let me get a whole speech out in one go until the last few days." She adopted a Jimmy-like poise. "Are you with me? It's the shape and the feel of the language I'm after, Pussy, do you see?" she said quietly in Jimmy's voice.

I giggled despite myself. It was a very well-observed impersonation. "Did he really call you Pussy?" I asked incredulously.

"Oh yes, he does that. Thankfully not often. Men and women. It's his version of 'darling'. The cliché is for theatricals to call each other darling. With Jimmy it's 'pussy'. Silly bugger. Take him with a pinch of salt and you'll be alright."

Take him with a pinch of salt. Duncan's advice again.

"I don't suppose you know a guy called Duncan Ward do you?" I asked.

"Duncan Ward. No, I don't think so, why?"

"He was my stage management tutor at college. Tipped me the wink about this job. That's what he said as well. About Jimmy." I still hadn't actually called him Mr Knowles, either to his face, or in conversation. "Apparently Duncan was an actor once and did a panto here."

"Do you know which one?"

"Not sure. He was one of the brokers' men in something or other, maybe fifteen years ago."

"*Rapunzel*," said Eleanor. "That was the one with the brokers' men. What's he like?"

I described Duncan. "Stocky, a bit chubby without being fat. Boyish face."

Recognition dawned. Eleanor nodded knowingly. "Yes, of course. I know who you mean. He was very good. I wasn't in that one, but I saw it. Very funny and good at comic walks."

Another side to Duncan that I knew nothing about. Duncan Ward the actor. I would phone him later and tell him I knew his guilty secret.

Eleanor and I chatted while I did the tea-lady chores, then the others came in to grab their steaming mugs of tea and coffee. Trevor Knightsbridge was suddenly by my right shoulder. "Lynn, just to say I thought you did great."

"Thanks," I said, "you did too."

"No really, I mean it. I wasn't fishing for a compliment," said Trevor. The dark eyes seemed moist, and I was unnerved by his stare.

There was one of those sticky silences, when once compliments have been exchanged, there's nothing else to say. Trevor gave what I think he hoped was an encouraging smile that somehow didn't quite make it to his eyes, and went away.

"Praise from Caesar is praise indeed," commented John Murray. John was tall and thin with somewhat pointed features. "I think you may have proved the point that stage management can act." He gave me an avuncular wink and wandered over to a chair.

I was beginning to feel better about my efforts. At least some of my peers had noticed.

Before long Jimmy called everyone back. For the rest of the day I resumed the (at this stage, fairly boring) job of following the script, prompting where needed, but mostly making notes. Life would get more interesting when I had some lights to play with, props to set, and a show to run. At this point it was all just a bit dull.

Late afternoon and Derek came by with more bits and pieces for the set. Lengths of scaffolding that bolted together to form a frame for the central platform. Heavy-duty plywood that sat on top, and then lighter grade plywood around the sides. The whole thing would be about eighteen inches off the ground.

Steps either side. Space to crawl around beneath the stage, and an offset trapdoor.

"Jimmy, if we could get the set built now, it'd be chance to show everyone how it fits," said Derek.

"Good idea, now come on Pussy Brooksy, it's your job to muster the troops," said Jimmy.

The van took about half an hour to offload. Fair play to the others; I didn't really have to carry anything very much. Derek, Keith and John, Finlay and the two Trevors did all the heavy carrying. Eleanor and I took the lighter things, but mostly I made notes; what had been where in the van.

The light was fading in the sky, and as we finished offloading the van I noticed Old Bill, sitting by the door to Archie's cottage. Watching. With nothing more to unload, I went over to him.

"Hello Bill. It's kind of you to help, but the job's done now."

Bill nuzzled my hand as I stroked his head. I looked up and peered into the porch, where the door was still ajar. I pushed it and it swung lightly open. Dust everywhere.

"Hello," I called out. No answer. The place seemed unlived in. Deserted. Then I heard his voice.

"Sheelagh?"

Suddenly I felt like I was intruding. What was I thinking of? This was a sweet old guy who I'd only met the once. He was that old he'd probably have forgotten who I was, and I was about to scare him to death.

"No, it's me. Brooke. We met yesterday."

Archie walked with that very smooth walk into the small hallway with the kitchen to the left, from where, through a very grimy window, you could see the hall.

"What an unexpected pleasure my dear. How nice."

I smiled. "The door was open and Old Bill was sat there. Just thought I'd make sure you were OK."

"How charming. I'm agreeably well, thank you my dear. Have your rehearsals finished for the day?"

"No, not yet." Sudden realisation. "No, actually, I really need to get back, we're putting the set together. Must run, bye."

I charged back to the hall. My little encounter with Archie had probably taken no longer than a minute at the most, but I felt like I'd been skiving.

For the next hour, we put the set together, led by Derek, with Keith clearly a very able old hand at all this. Eleanor stood to one side trying to look willing, and to be honest, so did I. The scaffolding was a bit like putting together a giant Meccano set, all slotted together and tightened up with an Allen key. I had the Allen key, and went around tightening all the screws before the surface was put on. The lights and the dimmer board we put to one side.

"We'll set that lot up tomorrow," said Keith. "You did a good job of the mark-up Brooke," he went on. "It was absolutely spot on to the set model."

"Thanks," I said as quietly as I dared. I stole a glance at Jimmy, who fortunately was deep in discussion with Trevor. I didn't want to tell Keith that Jimmy had done it and that I had had nothing to do with it; I didn't want Derek to overhear and to find out that I hadn't done one of the most basic jobs at the start of rehearsals, and I certainly didn't need another sarcastic putdown from Mr Knowles.

"We'll make a DSM out of an actor yet," said Keith with his rumbling voice, and gave me a friendly pat on the back.

It was time to pack up for the day and by now my scene as Lady Anne from earlier had been long forgotten. I was just filling in for the 'real' actress.

That's life.

ARCHIE

Yesterday had been a red-letter day. Brooke, or young Sheelagh, as I'd started to think of her, had come to see me. She hadn't stayed long. I must have dropped off sometime in the afternoon. Suddenly there had been a voice. I must have been dozing, because I could swear it had been Sheelagh's.

She stayed for less than a minute. Just wanted to see I was 'OK'. The Americanism from the war years had now become so much part of English common parlance. Not that I was one to quibble. She had come to see me. And that was special.

I watched her through the window as she went back. I saw Old Bill, looking like he'd sat there for some time. Keeping watch.

The van was there from the theatre. They must have offloaded the lights and scenery. That could only mean one thing. The play would be playing here. I'd thought when I did the mark-up that the actors were just rehearsing here, and then going on tour. If I was right, this would be the first professional show since the days of The Hideaway. I didn't count the Cranton Oh players. They meant well, but had more enthusiasm than ability. They had no idea of the quality of the productions that were here when Sheelagh and I had run it as a theatre. But this was a pro show. And young Sheelagh was involved.

And so this morning I could hardly wait to get over there. Before everyone else. Before the day started. Before Old Bill came for his walk.

Back in The Hideaway Theatre days I'd never liked going back inside when an evening performance was finished. The audience had gone, the performance over, and the place felt dead. The worst was after a successful run had finished and sometimes the stage crew would begin the set strike half an hour after the last performance. I would always avoid that. It was necessary, but felt like indecent haste. The magic of the show, the excitement of the audience, the energy of the actors replaced by the almost irreverent destruction of the set amid the banging of hammers and the splintering of wood.

So even now, after many years, it was in the mornings, at the start of a new day, that I liked to revisit The Hideaway. And remember.

On this morning I could hardly contain my excitement. After starting the day with my usual fond look at the magnificent rhododendron bush, I took myself over to the door as quickly as I could, and feeling for all the world like I was five years old and just starting school, went through into the lobby, as nervously as I had done a whole lifetime ago when I'd started my schooldays in this very place.

I was right. The set was positioned right on top of the mark-up I'd put down on the floor only yesterday. 'My' throne upstage centre. I wished I'd been here to help put it up. A professional show here again. Even if it was organised by the Edwardian Palace.

The rest of the hall was empty. The chairs still stacked at the sides, along with the lights. Four Manfrotto lighting tripods were on the floor, and around them an assortment of lamps. Fresnels, Spotlights, and some of those Par Can lamps that sometimes make an awful screeching noise. Plastic boxes with wires, and a dimmer board.

It was still early. I had a lot to set up before rehearsals. Before Sheelagh arrived.

BROOKLYN

I awoke very quickly in my silent bedroom with spring sunlight lighting the room. It was so quiet and still that it felt like a Sunday. I suppose living in a place like this, most mornings feel this way. I reached for my iPhone and stared at it blankly. It stared back, equally blankly. I had forgotten to plug the charger in, and the battery had gone flat overnight.

With no idea what the time was, I switched on Radio 4 in time to catch the last bit of an interview between John Humphrys and some politician. Then "This is the *Today* programme on Radio Four. It's ten past eight."

I leapt out of bed like it was on fire. This morning I'd decided to get there extra early. With rehearsals starting at ten, if I could get there a whole hour before then I'd be sure to get there ahead of Mr Knowles. No way did I want Mr Knowles there before me a second time.

I must have wasted five minutes searching for my phone charger before remembering that I'd taken it from my bag yesterday during the rehearsal. It must be still on the table at the hall.

Breakfast was the usual brief pleasantries with Beth Churchill, who proudly showed me some flyers for the show. As one of the Edwardian Palace's registered landladies for actors' digs it meant that she got two free tickets and a fistful of flyers to hand around to her friends who lived locally. Jimmy Knowles knew how to turn a penny, I'd give him that. Old Bill sat watching me from his basket by the door. Whenever I saw Bill he seemed to be waiting and watching. Either here in Beth's kitchen, or at the hall, or waiting for Archie to take him for a walk. Or maybe it was Bill taking Archie for a walk. I smiled. Oddly enough, that seemed quite likely. Two old friends who meet by mutual consent and neither could really tell whose idea it was in the first place.

I cleaned my teeth and got myself ready to start the day, and at twenty to nine I found myself walking down the garden path looking behind me to make sure Bill wasn't following. What was that about? Did I seriously think that the old dog had been trying to tell me something the day before? Clearly I did, much as I didn't want to admit it. And I was halfway to the hall before I realised that the idea of taking the shortcut through the woods hadn't even crossed my mind.

I was in luck. No dark green Ford Focus on the driveway; therefore no Jimmy. I fumbled for my key to the building that Derek had given me. I was clearly never destined to meet the enigmatic keyholder, Martin Helgin. Probably a village hall committee member. Incredibly, the door was unlocked. Again. Somebody needs to get their head around security. Or maybe down here, away from London, people don't bother so much.

I walked in and stopped in my tracks. The lighting stands which we'd laid on the floor and had decided to set up today, were all in position, crossbars clamped into the Doughty clamps, and lamps all looking very much like they'd been positioned and focussed. The table had been repositioned facing the stage, and another one put up beside it with the dimmer board all plugged in ready to go. A closed MacBook next to it, which I presumed was to be for the sound cues. That was the only thing not yet plugged in. Well, not quite. My phone charger was sat next to it.

Well, at least today I would have a head start in plotting some of the lighting cues. But who had done this? Whoever it was must have come back after we'd all left. But why? Why not just do it today like we'd said?

"Do you like your surprise?" The voice from the doorway gave me such a start I nearly swore. I spun round. Archie was standing in the doorway, with that faraway smile on his face.

"Oh, Archie, don't do that, you scared me to death." Actually, he really had. I sat down at the desk to recover.

"So sorry my dear. I wanted to surprise you."

"Well you certainly did that."

"No, I mean this." He gave a vague gesture around the room.

"Sorry, I don't understand." I could still feel my heart thumping.

"It's been a long time, but I think I put the plugs in the right holes. The stands were jolly heavy but once I'd got used to the little handle that you turn to raise the bar it wasn't so bad."

I could hardly believe what I was hearing. "You mean... *you* set the lights up?"

"Yes, my dear. And the dimmer board. All very complicated-looking but essentially the same idea as the ones we used to have."

"But..." I was dumbstruck. Somehow the idea of this very old man singlehandedly setting up a complete lighting rig overnight just didn't add up. "When did you do it?

"I still have a key. And I was up early this morning. I only finished maybe, I don't know, half an hour ago. I've been waiting for you to arrive."

"Oh... that's nice." Waiting for me to arrive. It was the sort of thing that, coming from creepy Trevor, would have been, well, creepy. But there was a childlike innocence to Archie, rather like a boy who has made some teacakes for his mum and wants approval. "Thank you for… doing my job for me." I smiled in what I hoped was an encouraging way.

"The pleasure, dear lady…" He paused and looked embarrassed. "I mean, it was an absolute joy. Nice to be back in the theatre."

An odd thought struck me. "I don't suppose you had anything to do with the stage being marked up so well yesterday morning?"

Archie chuckled. "Aha! Discovered! I wasn't sure whether to tell you or just let you work it out for yourself. Yes, dear lady, it was I with the tape, I with the lights, and I who made the throne."

I was feeling out of my depth in this conversation. I had been convinced that Jimmy had been here early and was fed up with me for being late, even when I hadn't been. Keith's observation about the accuracy of the mark-up had presumably been meant as encouragement to me; I'd not wanted Jimmy to overhear that exchange and make a sarcastic quip, when all the time it had been this increasingly strange old man. I was speechless. I sat there with what must have been a confused expression on my face.

"Well… thank you. I'll know who to ask if ever I need a good stage rigger," I managed at last.

Archie beamed.

I said, "Sorry… you said you *made* the throne?" I knew for a fact that the throne had come up from the Edwardian Palace scene dock. I'd helped Derek offload it from the van on day one. It was heavy enough for two to carry. Probably a good job that this old chap just had to drag it across the room to where it had been ready for rehearsal on the mark-up.

"Yes, I made it," said Archie simply. "It must be a good thirty years old. We used it for *Macbeth*; *Dick Whittington* – painted very different colours for each play of course. But yes, it's seen good service. Built it not far from where it now stands."

Again, I was out of my depth. "Right..." I said, trying to piece together all the bits of this very unlikely jigsaw. "So... you're something to do with the drama group here?" Again, given his age, that seemed unlikely, but maybe thirty years previously, village hall theatre might have been his thing.

Archie smiled his faraway smile again. "No, dear lady, come with me." He took a few steps toward the lobby and turned to me. "Just through here."

Completely mystified, I followed to where Archie stood looking at a photograph in a dark wood frame on the wall beside the box office.

"Look," he said, "that's me there." He pointed to an attractive young woman beside his much younger self. "And that's Sheelagh." The picture showed most of the front of the building in which we now stood. Over the doorway was a sign: *THE HIDEAWAY.* The figures were full-length and the photograph taken from maybe twenty feet away, but the man was unmistakeably Archie. The same piercing eyes in a much younger face.

"This was your theatre?" I asked in an awestruck whisper.

"It was." Archie turned to me and smiled a soft, wasn't-it-wonderful type of smile.

"Wow," was all I could manage. "And you... built the scenery and stuff?"

"Yes, I did. *We* did. In those days everyone mucked in together. Well, it was Sheelagh more than me. I was good at business; she was the artist. She chose the plays. Appeared in some of them. It was glorious."

"The throne?" I asked, my mind still playing catch-up.

"Yes. I can't tell you what pleasure it gave me to see it again. So glad it's still going to be used. Hit my thumb with a hammer when I built it. Hurt like hell and Sheelagh told me off for swearing." He chuckled.

"So how long ago did the theatre move from here to the Edwardian Palace?"

"It never did, dear lady. We closed down. The Palace took over. Took our stock of costumes and props, but that was the end of The Hideaway." Archie added sadly: "Actually, it finished before then really. When Sheelagh died. After she went, I knew it was over. I loved it for her, you see. The theatre was her world, and anyway, I was starting to get old. The place was an empty shell after Sheelagh went, and then, well, a big party was thrown in my honour. Jimmy Knowles made a speech. Votes of thanks and all that, but everyone knew the place had died some years before. All very nice and 'Isn't Archie a good chap?' But we all knew it was over."

There were tears in his eyes when he said that. I sensed he really wanted to talk. I still had a few minutes before anyone started to arrive.

"Tell me more," I said.

We sat down in the hall by the dimmer board on the table and Archie told me his story. How he'd left the navy after the war. A second lieutenant who'd seen active service, had been shot at, torpedoed, but yet had survived. How after a brief career in Fleet Street, he had met his wife and how, on a whim, had ended up buying this place. He had brought Sheelagh to the village where he'd grown up and had shown her what in his youth had been the village school. This place. He and Sheelagh had been a very effective team and had turned a former school hall into an atmospheric and intimate theatre running mostly weekly and sometimes fortnightly repertory seasons during the summer, and a fairly full programme for most of the rest of the year. He was describing a world that was now long gone. Almost from the days when actors would meet in Crewe on a Sunday, accompanying their trunks with their costumes to the next job.

"In those days we did everything. Actors weren't averse to painting scenery if it was needed. We'd often burn the midnight oil working on the set," said Archie. "Exhausting work for them. The actors would rehearse during the day for a show going on the following week, and meanwhile would be performing every night. Never quite knew how they remembered the lines, but Sheelagh always said it was just practice. Actors would often start as assistant stage managers. Like you're doing. Then they'd get an acting role if they were lucky. That happened here many times. It was the way it worked in those days." Archie paused, looking into the middle distance. "It wouldn't have been for me. Acting. Can't even remember how old I am, let alone lines."

I laughed. I felt I could listen to this wonderful old man all day. "How old are you? If it's not a rude question," I added.

"No idea, Brooke." Archie thought for a moment. "I was thirty when I came out of the Navy, and that was in '46."

I quickly did the maths. Surely not. "So you were born in… 1916?"

"Yes, I suppose I was, but I was very young at the time."

"But…" I couldn't quite believe what I was saying. "That makes you ninety-eight!"

"Yes…" Archie paused. "I suppose it does. What year is this?"

"It's 2014." I giggled, sure he was winding me up. But I realised he wasn't.

"Ah, believe me, when you get older you do forget silly things like that," said Archie. "Probably why the Queen sends out telegrams when you reach a hundred. Just to remind people how old they are. Or maybe it's a case of 'Come in number five, your time is up.'"

We both chuckled. I liked Archie enormously. He was an odd mix. He looked very frail and wispy, but was a natural raconteur, still had a sharp mind, and was apparently still able to rig a set of lights.

"Well, you must come and see this show," I said; "we open a week on Saturday. I'm sure they'll give you a comp."

"I wouldn't bank on that," said Archie. "Young Mr Knowles doesn't tend to give comps. I'm quite happy to pay anyway. As a producer it's quite irritating when you're trying to make it pay and people want comps. It'll be the first play I've seen here since the glory days, so to speak. Seven thirty start I'm guessing?"

"Eight," I corrected him, and the reminder of time suddenly gave me a fright. I had been so immersed in Archie's story of The Hideaway Theatre that I'd lost track of the time. Not only that, but still nobody had arrived for the rehearsal. Despite finding my phone charger, I hadn't plugged it or my iPhone in. "Archie, I'm sorry," I said, "I've lost track of the time a bit, I really should be getting on."

"Not at all my dear, it's time Bill and I were going for our walk. He'll be waiting."

My iPhone still didn't have enough power to start up, so, in a reflection of Archie's own old-fashioned politeness, I walked with him through the lobby to where I could see Old Bill waiting patiently by Archie's front door. The dog saw Archie coming towards him, and plodded gently towards him, his tail wagging and shoulders quivering with excitement.

I walked back to my phone, which had now just about finished switching itself back on. I cursed my forgetfulness for not charging it last night. Just twenty to ten, which was probably about the time I'd have finished setting up if Archie hadn't done it for me. I had been talking with him for over forty-five minutes.

Where on earth was everyone? Five missed calls. Two texts. One from Scott with another of his cheery good mornings. The other from a number I didn't recognise but instinctively knew was the Edwardian Palace Theatre. Derek: *Brooke, call me or Gemma ASAP.*

Two voicemail messages; message one received at 9.02 am: "Hello Brooke, this is Gemma at the theatre. Hope you get this message in time. Jimmy's wanting a later start this morning so can you contact all the actors and tell them to get in for ten thirty? However, he'd like to see you there at ten."

Followed by another in a more irritable tone at 9.34 am: "Brooke, it's Gemma again, can you call me as soon as you get this message? Jimmy's not best pleased at the moment. He wants to see you at the Institute for ten. The rest of the cast for ten thirty."

I started to feel slightly sick. *Jimmy's not best pleased.* My happy mood of a few minutes earlier had evaporated like a mist.

I phoned Derek but his phone went straight to voicemail. I tried to keep my voice as light as possible. "Derek, it's Brooke. I'm sorry, I've only just got your text… er… call me back when you get this. Bye."

I'm ashamed to say my hand was trembling as I pressed the numbers for Gemma's office. I'd only met Gemma briefly, but she was Jimmy's theatre and finance manager. Like Derek, she seemed to have learned to cope with his ways. She was in her forties, and I had the impression she didn't suffer fools gladly. Possibly the hard shell was something she'd had to develop in order to cope with Mr Knowles.

"Hi Gemma, it's Brooklyn."

"Ah, there you are, we've been trying to contact you," said Gemma, haughtily stating the obvious.

"Sorry," I said. *Apologising again!* "I've only just picked up your messages. What's going on?"

"It's probably best if Jimmy tells you that himself. He's on his way."

"Right… OK then… no problem. Thanks Gemma," I said as lightly as I could manage, and ended the call. A line from *Richard III*, spoken by Lady Anne, came into my mind: *Besides, he hates me, and will no doubt shortly be rid of me.*

This job had not really gone well so far. The job itself was OK. The other actors seemed alright, even if the leading man did seem a bit creepy, but Mr Knowles had treated me in such a way that I felt undervalued, incompetent and largely unnoticed. It now looked like I was going to be fired. *Jimmy's not best pleased… It's probably best if Jimmy tells you that himself.* No matter which way I thought of it, a private interview with a boss who clearly didn't much like me, when he was 'not best pleased', didn't look promising.

Well, sod him. Sod him and his stupid pretensions. Talking with Archie earlier had given me an insight into how theatre managers should be. Tremendous energy and drive, enough to still have some of it left at ninety-eight years of age. Unfailingly courteous and a natural gentleman.

My phone rang. Now what? Without looking, I answered it.

"Brooklyn darling, how are you?" The superficial bonhomie from Crispin McLaren, my agent, was really not what I wanted to hear just then.

"Hi Crispin, what's up?" I asked, perhaps a little curtly.

"Good news precious, and I'm really hoping you're going to say yes, because I've put my head on the block a bit for you on this one."

"Go on then," I prompted.

"The BBC want you for *Crimewatch*. They've cast this one from headshots and they've had a look at your showreel on Spotlight."

"OK, sounds good, what is it, and where?"

"It's one of their reconstructions, and they want you because you're a very close match for the murder victim. You probably saw it on the news."

Suddenly I knew what Crispin was going to say. "You mean that girl who died down near here?"

"Yes, that's right darling. Awful, and I do hope you're taking care of yourself. That's the other thing. You're down there anyway, and it's a night shoot. Not very much, really. Mostly just walking the route where the girl was last seen."

"Oh… Crispin, wow, that's a bit spooky."

"Course it is sweetie, but really it's money for old rope, and it's a TV credit, and it's good money."

"OK. So when is it?"

"Dates aren't yet set in stone, but it's either next Thursday night or the following Monday. Either way, the show goes out Thursday of the week after."

"Right. Yeah, OK…" I said, my mind racing. Next Thursday was to be our technical day. Who's to say what time we would finish? The Monday would be better. The show would have opened on the Saturday and then Sunday and Monday were to be days off. Of course the Thursday might not be a problem anyway if I was about to be fired. Sod it. Take control. "Crispin, OK, tell them yes. And tell them if they want me that badly it'll have to be the Monday, because I'll be tech-ing all day Thursday."

"Alright sweetie, will do. Speak soon. Byeeeeee!"

It felt like my head was spinning. In under four days my life had gone from 'Don't walk through the woods' to 'Darling, can you recreate the last known movements of the murder victim?' It was a work offer, but it was hard to feel much joy about it. Not at all the sort of job I would tell my friends about and enjoy their congratulations, and OK, being honest, their envy.

I decided I would tell no one. For the time being I would put it out of my mind. Besides, in this business nothing is certain anyway until you've signed on the dotted line.

The sound of a car outside. The slam of a door. Another. A third. First into the hall was Derek. Then Keith Groat. Each with blank expressions, and an air of an important announcement. Then Jimmy.

"There you are Brooklyn." It was the first time he'd used my name properly. "Take a seat."

I sat down behind the lighting desk, feeling like a young offender seeing a probation officer.

Derek had arranged three chairs opposite me. It was then that I knew I was going to be fired. *Besides he hates me, and will no doubt shortly be rid of me.*

"Now Brooklyn," said Mr Knowles after a pause. "First of all, the best way to annoy your employer is not to answer your bloody phone when they want to speak with you urgently.

"Yes, Mr Knowles, sorry, my battery died overnight."

Jimmy went on as if he hadn't heard me. "It would seem that Miss Powell has decided to relinquish the joys of working with me for the glitzy glamour of Hollywood, so she won't be returning today, or indeed ever."

That was so not what I was expecting to hear that I must have just stared back blankly.

"So I've decided to pluck you from the ranks of dank obscurity and give you a chance to do some more of what you did yesterday. I'd like you to take over the role of Lady Anne."

"Lady Anne?" I replied, stupidly.

"Yes, you remember Lady Anne, the one you made such a good job of yesterday," said Mr Knowles. "Then later on you also get to play Catesby, and Richard's mother."

"Well…" I was stuck for words. This man of whom I was still quite scared, who a few moments earlier I was convinced was going to yell at me just before he fired me, was now offering me an acting job in a role I'd always wanted. What's more, he thought that yesterday I had 'made such a good job of it'.

Keith Groat and Derek were watching me closely.

"I think the word you're searching for is yes," said Mr Knowles.

"Wow… yes of course, I'd love to," I said, feeling tears start to well up. Partly I think through relief, but mostly through joyous surprise.

"Good," he said. "Made myself unpopular with Pussy Groat here and Derek, but they'll get over it."

I smiled weakly. "I don't under—"

"It means that you won't be running the show. Derek will be doing that most nights, and then on the few he can't do, the responsibility will be shared between you and Keith here."

"Oh I see, right," I said. My head was in a whirl. The *Crimewatch* job, which a few minutes before had seemed almost like a consolation for losing this job, now seemed something of a mild inconvenience. I would infinitely prefer to be in a theatre show than on television, even if it was with the notorious Mr Knowles.

"Good that's settled then," he said, and actually smiled.

"Well… thank you," I stammered, "and Keith, Derek, thank you too for helping to make this happen."

"Don't thank them Brooksy, they do as they're bloody well told," said Mr Knowles with a chuckle.

Derek and Keith gave a polite laugh, and with that the interview seemed to be over. We stood up, and partly for something to say and partly because I needed some space to think, I said I'd make the tea. Derek and Keith drifted outside to get some air, possibly for a quick fag before rehearsals but more likely to meet the others as they arrived and give them the gossip. Mr Knowles sat down and flicked through his script.

"And Brooklyn, one other thing…" he said sternly.

"Mr Knowles?" I replied.

Over his shoulder he said, "You can call me Jimmy." And then he went back to his script.

***

As I'd thought, news of my promotion had reached the others before they came into the hall, so Jimmy Knowles' official announcement was unnecessary. The others all smiled their congratulations. Trevor just registered the news and then avoided my eyes. I was still trying to get my head around everything that had happened: the long conversation with Archie about how things had been in the days of The Hideaway Theatre; about how in those days a young actor at the start of their career would be doing ASM duties, then they would get a part. That was the way it worked in those days. And now, here, it had happened to me. Rachel Powell's sudden decision not to come back. Presumably phone calls from the formidable Con Covington late yesterday afternoon or even early this morning. Rachel therefore must have a fighting chance of getting the role in whatever film franchise it was, and had thought it was worth terminating her contract here. A huge, and for someone like me, career-threatening decision. But Rachel was older. More experience. More contacts. A better agent. Then there was *Crimewatch*, if it happened at all. I decided to put that to one side of my mind for the present.

Ironically, now that I was 'the proper actress', in Jimmy-speak, I spent the first couple of hours of the rehearsal going through the stage manager's script with Derek, and in whispers, passing everything on to him that I'd noted down the previous couple of days. Keith looked on when he wasn't needed for a scene.

Then I opened the new Penguin edition of *Richard III* that Jimmy had brought with him from the theatre, and began marking in the cuts and putting a small pencilled > sign next to any lines to be spoken by me. Time to start learning the lines. The fact that I already knew the play quite well would be an advantage. But there was no time to lose. Jimmy was working on the Clarence murder scene, so I went outside into the lobby and started slowly pacing up and down, memorising the lines. Might as well start at the beginning. *Set down, set down your honourable load…* The outside door was open, the morning bright with crisp spring sunlight, and I slowly wandered up and down, saying the lines to myself, imagining Trevor's reaction, then speaking my next line and so on. Further down the path I noticed the matronly figure of Eleanor Boscombe doing the same thing. For non-theatre people, this must be a strange sight: actors pacing thoughtfully around holding a book and apparently talking to themselves.

Then I saw Archie, with his slow, graceful walk, coming up the path past Eleanor. She was so into her part that she ignored Archie's friendly nod in her direction. I smiled at him as he came towards me and I walked with him for the ten yards or so to his front door.

"Method actress," he said with a twinkle in his sharp eyes. "So into her part she just looked straight through me."

I laughed. "She's actually very nice," I said, and feeling like a little girl telling her grandfather that she's come top of the class in a school test, I told Archie my news about being given an acting part after only a couple of days in stage management.

"That's simply splendid Brooke. I'm very, very pleased for you, I really am."

"So you'll have to come and see the show now," I said.

"I absolutely shall my dear. Eleanor's very good by the way. I saw her do Lady Bracknell at the Edwardian Palace. You'll learn a lot from her," said Archie. "And you've got young Trevor in the cast, I notice."

"What, you mean Trevor Knightsbridge?"

"Yes, I saw him the other day and hardly recognised him. He's changed so much over the years."

I was surprised at this. I hadn't thought that Archie would know any of my new colleagues. But why wouldn't he? The theatre is a small world.

Archie went on to say, "He was always very serious. Rather shy. His parents used to bring him here a lot when he was a boy. Long time ago now. Then he went off to London and did his training. I haven't seen him now for... well... after our conversation this morning my dear, I wouldn't like to say how many years." Archie smiled, and then said sincerely, "Brooke, my dear, I can't tell you how glad I am to have met you, and

I'm not sure if I should tell you this, but you know, you're so like Sheelagh when she was younger."

I remembered the old photograph Archie had shown me that morning; the young woman standing outside The Hideaway Theatre. To be honest, I really couldn't see the likeness. Vaguely similar hairstyle I suppose, but the bob has been fashionable for decades, from Clara Bow to Twiggy and beyond.

"You old charmer," I said in what I hoped was a charming way.

"Well, a bit in looks, but also with your enthusiasm for the profession. Sheelagh had that. It's a wonderful thing to see," he said with that faraway smile.

Archie went into his house. Presumably Bill would by now be back at Beth Churchill's, chomping away at a bowl of dog food. I decided that if Beth didn't need her second complimentary ticket, I would give it to Archie.

Back to the lines.

***

That night up in my room at Beth's I'd spent a good hour and a half making phone calls. The first, of course, was to Scott.

"Brooklyn that's brilliant," he said simply. "I'll see if I can find a copy of York Notes on eBay."

"You won't need to; if it's done well, then you'll understand it."

"Yes dear," he said with a chuckle. Despite the fact that he'd thoroughly enjoyed our first-date trip to *Hamlet*, and despite having me as a girlfriend, somehow the notion that Shakespeare was not accessible still lurked in his mind. Then I told him about the *Crimewatch* possibility and I could hear the change in his voice.

"That's a bit creepy. Are you sure you're OK with that?"

"Yes… I think so. I thought it was a bit creepy too, but it's work, it's TV and it's filming down here."

"Yeah that's kind of the point," said Scott. "You're there, in the place where it happened, and you look like this Lynn Arthur girl. It's all a bit too much like tempting fate."

I realised that I actually knew very little about this murder that had happened so nearby. Life seemed to have been so full lately that I hadn't properly listened to the news. "Is that her name? I must admit I didn't know."

"Brook…lyn," he said, separating the syllables of my name in a tone of mild reproof, "when did you last hear the news? I know you're outside London, but you're not on the moon. She was found in the woods near Cranton Overleigh with a cracked skull. That's kind of why I said not to walk through the woods."

I'd started to bristle at Scott's tone, but then the seriousness hit me. What had happened was awful. And it had happened here. I'd been so self-preoccupied that I'd scarcely given it a thought other than mild annoyance at Beth for being overprotective on that first morning, and even at Old Bill, who had, in his doggy way, persuaded me not to take that shortcut. Dogs are supposed to sense things that humans can't: you know, hear higher notes and stuff. Maybe it was true.

All I had seen were newspaper pictures on the tube, and I'd vaguely heard a news report the other morning, while I'd been dreaming about Jimmy and his annoying "Right then stage manager, are we set up?"

"Do you think I shouldn't do it?" I asked.

"I dunno… I don't like it," said Scott. "It's just a bit… well… I dunno."

I agreed. I think. Or did I? I'm an actor, and that means you are paid to act. You don't have to always like the parts you're asked to play. You just do the job. If you don't want to, then fine, so go and work in a supermarket, but don't bleat about not liking a job. Despite all that, there was still something about this that made me uncomfortable too. Trying to rationalise it, I told myself that doing this reconstruction may help to catch the killer; that my being down here anyway was just coincidence. It still just felt… wrong.

"Besides," I said, trying to lighten the mood between us, "it may not happen anyway. I'm only available on the Monday and I've told Crispin to tell them it's then or never."

"Well let's hope it's never," said Scott seriously.

We talked some more, then did our usual signing off.

"Love you, Blondie."

"Love you, Brooklyn."

"Downtown!"

But there was still something unresolved. Something we'd nearly argued about, despite the fact that we both agreed on it.

The next call was to Mum and Dad. Dad was his usual quiet self. Mum was effusive. When, as a teenager, I'd announced that I wanted to act for a living, I'd had the type of conversations that most young actors have with their parents. Why not go to university, get a degree, get a steady job, and so on. Once they'd got used to the idea, I think Mum wanted to imagine me in musical theatre; but credit where it's due, she couldn't have been more supportive about my wanting to do classical theatre and 'proper' acting, and now that I'd landed such a great part, she said what she'd also said when she came to see me in *The Seagull*: "Just so long as I won't need a degree to understand it."

Next I phoned Duncan Ward. It went straight to voicemail, so instead of leaving a message, I went back to the script. Lines.

It wasn't until nearly eleven that I got through to Duncan. He'd been on his follow-spot job for *Phantom*. By this point I was in bed getting ready to turn the light out.

"That's great Brooke," he said when I told him my news. "Like I said, he's a bit old-school, but this is part of that mindset that's good." He put on a mock Jimmy-voice. "All actors should bloody well learn to stage-manage," and then in his normal voice, added, "but only two days in is going it some."

"Also, I've found out a bit about your sordid past," I said.

"What do you mean?"

"Oh, I dunno… just a rumour I've heard about a brokers' man in *Rapunzel* with a nifty ability at funny walks."

"Nooooooooooo!" said Duncan. "Who told you that?"

"Eleanor Boscombe and Derek Leonard."

"Well bugger me," said Duncan, "how is Eleanor?"

"She seems OK. We had a chat sometime yesterday after I'd read in for the girl who left."

"Yeah she's alright, is Eleanor. Done a lot of stuff for Jimmy down the years. She wasn't in *Rapunzel*, but she lives down that way somewhere. And Derek, well, I suppose I should have told him to keep his big trap shut." He laughed.

"So how come you were acting?" I asked, more bluntly than I intended.

"Well, I like to think I was," said Duncan, laughing. I could hear the sound of the pub in the background. "I tried it for a bit, but I was never very good to be honest. Just can't do the deep stuff at all. Watching you lot at college doing Chekhov and the heavy stuff: I just couldn't do that. It's just not in me, and I reached a point where I thought: D'you know what? I could just carry on, and only ever be a mediocre actor, or I could go down a different route and be an excellent stage manager. So that's what I did."

"That's great," I said, weakly.

"I think that brokers' man job might have been the last part I played. I then stage-managed for Jimmy for a bit, you know, helping Derek out now and then; and then I came back to London. How are you getting on with Jimmy?"

"OK I think. I'm still feeling my way a bit with him. He made me call him Mr Knowles for the first couple of days, but now he's made me an actress I'm allowed to call him Jimmy."

"Does he still call people Pussy?" asked Duncan.

"Oooh yes. Couldn't believe that when I heard it. D'you know Keith Groat?"

"No, don't think so."

"Well, Jimmy called him Pussy Groat to his face. Unbelievable."

"Oh yes, been there, had that," said Duncan. "The only thing is, when he called me 'Pussy Ward', I came straight back at him and said it sounded like a ladies' clap clinic, and everybody else fell about laughing. I'd never have dared if I'd thought about it first, but he never called me that again."

I laughed.

Duncan said, "The thing is, Jimmy's used to getting his own way. Military background sometime way back when. Then he came out of the army and went into theatre, so he brings a certain style with him. But that's the result of a posh school and a regimented background. A lot of it comes from the fact that he admired the guy who ran the old theatre in Cranton Overleigh."

"Archie Stephens?" I asked, amazed that Duncan knew Archie.

"Yes, that's him. Amazing guy. Tremendous energy. I didn't really know him, but I used to see him around the Eddy Palace after the Hideaway Theatre closed. Natural gent. He was the real thing. Genuine old school. Jimmy's more of a modern imitation. Like a mock antique."

"Duncan, that's amazing—" I'd started to say, when Duncan interrupted.

"Brooke, I've got to go love, I'm meeting someone for a drink and they've just arrived."

"That's OK, but—"

"Yeah look, tell you what, email me a show schedule and I'll try and catch the show on tour."

"OK Duncan, will do. Bye."

I ended the call. Even better, I would get Duncan to come down to see opening night, and reacquaint him with Archie. I had the kind of feeling when you've just bought a present for a friend and can't wait to give it to them. Reintroducing Duncan to Archie after so many years.

I was getting tired now but just before turning out the light, I surfed the web on my iPhone.

Lynn Arthur.

Police are still investigating the death of twenty-three-year-old Lynn Arthur from Bournemouth. Miss Arthur was originally from London but had moved down to the south coast a year before she died. She was last seen on CCTV after leaving her job in a bar in Port St Catherine, and then was found dead the following morning in Forgers Wood, a two square mile nature reserve between Cranton Overleigh and Dunslinton.

The face of the dead girl looked back at me. A 'selfie' taken in a bar somewhere. She did look a bit like me if you thought about it. Clearly the BBC had thought about it. Probably not something I should be thinking about before going to sleep. A bit like watching a horror film before bed. Why do people do that? I prefer an episode of *Friends.*

I surfed onto Facebook. On a whim I searched for Rachel Powell. Four appeared. One was a lady in her fifties, another was a black girl, a third was in California, and then there was the young woman I'd met the other day.

I nearly didn't bother, but something in me felt I should thank her for being the reason I got a job, so I sent her a friend request and wrote a quick message: *Hi Rachel; I owe you. Thanks for dropping out of R3: I'm now playing your role and loving it. Hope your auditions etc. go really well for you. Brooke.*

My eyelids feeling really heavy, I turned out the light.

ARCHIE

Another thing about growing old: you start to wonder how much longer you've got, and what it will be like when you go. What happens? Do you just fall asleep? If there is an afterlife, are you able to look back and say, "Ah yes, that was the day I died"? Do you suddenly become young again? Or is it just a case of 'lights fade to black' and that's it? *Good night sweet Prince, and flights of angels sing thee to thy rest. The rest is silence.*

Forever.

So many questions. No answers.

After my long talk with Brooke, I went for my usual walk with Old Bill plodding along beside me. So glad she liked her surprise. So glad that I could still manage to rig lights at my age. Ninety-eight. *Ninety-eight?* Really? The arithmetic was incontrovertible. Born in 1916. It's now 2014. Therefore I'm ninety-eight. But I don't feel it. I feel like I'm old, yes. Even very old. But ninety-eight? Looking at Old Bill, I wondered which of us was older. Someone told me once you have to multiply dog years by seven to get the equivalent age in human years. On that basis Bill must be in his nineties as well. Two old codgers walking through the woods.

During the past few days I've felt younger and more alive than I have in years. Professional theatre back in The Hideaway. My theatre.

And Brooke. That lovely young girl, so very like Sheelagh at the same age. Had I gone too far telling her that? She'd seemed embarrassed. I hate to admit it, but I was a little in love with her. Not in a dirty old man kind of way. More like a favourite uncle to a niece. So full of life. Pretty. And smart. Most of all, she seemed to like me. When one is in one's eighties – oh, very well, nineties – the youngsters don't often pay much attention. Even those in their fifties are youngsters. Even someone like Jimmy Knowles is still, compared to me, a youngster. But Brooke had come to see me. Then when I'd come back from my walk with Old Bill we'd talked again. I told her what I thought of that Eleanor woman. Always was a bit superior, that one. So obsessed with her deep characterisations that she wouldn't notice you if you dressed up in a silly hat and said boo. Just like today. So self-absorbed. Not like Brooke.

I would go and see the first night. Time to dig the suit out of the mothballs. It should still fit. I have the kind of metabolism that allowed me to eat more or less anything and never put on an ounce. Sheelagh used to say I was like a greyhound.

For the first pro show at the Old Hideaway, I would wear a black bow tie and evening suit and take my seat in the stalls and watch the show. And Brooke.

BROOKLYN

You very quickly get into a routine when you're away from home and on your own. Get up, breakfast, check phone for messages. Always one from Scott. Check Facebook. No reply to my friend request to Rachel. Oh well. A new friend request. Trevor Knightsbridge. I very nearly hit 'not now', which really means 'not ever', but on an impulse I pressed 'accept'. The guy did seem a bit intense, but I was working with him and anyway, I'm always careful about what I put out there in cyberspace. I could always delete him if he started getting weird.

Walk to work with Old Bill plodding along beside me. Talk to Archie. Today there were no surprises in store. After the past couple of days I almost expected him to have arranged the chairs in advance of the performance. This morning he was just standing outside the front door enjoying the morning air and waiting for Old Bill. He gave me a friendly wave.

"Morning Archie," I said.

"Good morning my dear. I trust you slept well." It was the sort of thing you imagine a butler saying in *Upstairs, Downstairs.*

"Yes thanks," I said. "I must tell you this: I was talking to a friend last night who knows you."

"Really my dear? How extraordinary."

"Yes, in fact he's my stage management tutor from college, and it's partly due to him that I got this job in the first place."

"Go on."

"Well, I phoned him last night to tell him my news – you know, about getting the Lady Anne part. Somehow we got to talking about you, and he said he remembered seeing you at the Edwardian Palace."

Archie's face clouded a bit. "Really? What is the gentleman's name?"

"Duncan. Duncan Ward." He used to be an actor and was in a pantomime as one of the brokers' men in *Rapunzel*.

Recognition dawned on Archie's face. "Ah yes. *Rapunzel*. That was in the first season after the real theatre closed. Young Jimmy Knowles was kind enough to let me hang around the place. Duncan Ward…" Archie screwed up his eyes in concentration. "Don't think I remember him. I wasn't directly involved in any of the productions then. I just used to hang around and enjoy the atmosphere."

"Apparently he was quite good at comic walks," I said.

"Ah yes… I think I do know who you mean. Tubby-looking boyish lad?"

"Yes that's him," I said. "Duncan and I were talking about how actors would sometimes start in stage management, and that led on to talking about, well, the old-school tradition, and Duncan said that you were the real thing."

"Did he now?" Archie smiled vaguely.

Suddenly afraid I might have said too much, I quickly added, "He also said you had amazing energy."

Archie laughed. "Not so much now as I did."

"I don't know so much about that," I said. I was still amazed that this sprightly ninety-eight-year-old could still rig lights single-handed.

"The theatre world is a very small one my dear. You'll find that. I just hope you have as much fun in it as I did."

Somehow that seemed a natural end to the conversation, so I said, "Have a nice day" to Archie and went on ahead into the hall, using my own key for the first time.

Inside was full of early morning stillness. Well, 9.30 is early morning in theatre. I love silence sometimes. This place had tremendous atmosphere, and even though it now looked more like a multi-function village hall, it still had the feel of the theatre about it. Archie's influence was still here, even though The Hideaway was long gone.

***

"Hi Crispin," I said. It was lunchtime and no sooner had I turned my phone onto 'normal' from 'silent' than the call came through.

I had the feeling familiar to all actors on getting a call from their agent. It's usually good news; the worst is when they don't call at all. It also often involves a hurried change of plan, often along the lines of 'Can you get to a commercial casting tomorrow morning at ten?' Of course, if you want to maintain credibility as an actor the answer has to be 'yes' as often as possible, but that usually involves having to ask for time off from whatever temp job you're doing, and that's not always easy. Do it too often, and you piss off your employer and then you can't pay the rent. This wasn't one of those calls, but I had a sneaky idea of what was coming. A change of plan.

"Brooke sweetie, the Beeb have been on and they definitely want you for the *Crimewatch* shoot."

"OK, great," I said, hoping I was striking the right balance between sounding pleased and being noncommittal. "When is it?"

"Well darling, I told them your availability, and they're happy to use you on the Monday."

"That's a relief."

"Yes, originally they wanted the Friday but I told them you were working and couldn't possibly do it then. I was quite pleased to do that, to be honest. At least we don't look desperate. Anyway, it's an evening shoot like I said, but there really isn't much. It's just shots of you leaving the place where this girl worked, then to where she was last seen, and then as Sondheim would say, it's *Into the Woods* for the shots near the murder scene. I can't see it taking more than a few hours. I think you'll be tucked up in bed by midnight."

"Right… great. Thanks Crispin. I suppose I should let them know down here."

"Yes, you can do, but I was going to do that anyway."

Suddenly I remembered I hadn't told Crispin my news about getting an acting role. I filled him in quickly. There was an awkward silence.

"Well, darling that's great, but I do wish you'd told me first."

"Yes… sorry." *Apologising again*. "It all happened so quickly, I just didn't think to."

"Well sweetie, you really should have. Listen: have you signed anything?"

"No, not yet." I felt like a teenager in trouble for not handing in homework.

"Well don't. Not until I've seen a copy."

"Listen, Crispin, really, I don't want to rock the boat; I think this could be a really good job, and I don't want to upset them."

"Yes sweetie I know that, but this is business, and that's why you pay me commission."

I was starting to think that I might be in trouble with both my employer and my agent. "Well, yes, I know that…" I must have sounded uncertain.

"Look, don't worry darling, I'll tread carefully, but tell me: have you discussed money at all?"

"No, not at all," I said.

"Good. Right answer. The thing is sweetie, I think they should pay you more than you were getting for being the ASM and general gopher. I'll see what I can do. Speak soon, bye love." He ended the call.

Crispin was right of course. The truth was that I was so glad to be offered an acting role that I hadn't even considered that there might be more money involved. I had a lot to learn still. Somewhere in my head there was still the slight surprise that I would be getting paid at all. All my previous acting experience had been shows at college and before that, school plays and am-dram stuff.

It was only then that I noticed that Finlay Beckett and Trevor George were munching their sandwiches nearby. Trevor George was the sort of guy who looked like an accountant. Glasses, balding pate and always wearing a jacket, where he kept his script in the hip pocket, and Finlay was fresh-faced with a close-cropped beard and a mop of brown hair, and liked to wear loose-fitting sweaters.

"Your agent?" Trevor George asked.

"Yes."

"So who are you with?" he asked.

"Crispin McLaren."

"Oh right," said Trevor vaguely. "Any good?"

"Yes, he's OK I guess. I've been seen for a couple of things. *Holby City* a little while ago, but I didn't get it."

"Half the battle is getting seen," he said.

This was sounding like the conversation I'd had with Rachel. The truth was that I'd had that casting for *Holby City* and had done a couple of corporate training videos, and that had been pretty much it since leaving college. Apart from *The*

Seagull straight after graduating. What I was doing now was talking it up. And a *Holby City* casting sounded good, even though I hadn't got the job.

I didn't want my *Crimewatch* news to be generally known just yet, so before either Trevor George or Finlay could probe any further, I asked, "So, who are you with, Trevor?"

"Con Covington."

"Oh right, so the same as Rachel then."

"Yeah," he said a little ruefully. "Rachel. New kid on the block and now she's casting for Paramount or someone. I dunno..."

"New kid on the block?" I asked. I'd formed the impression that Rachel, in her early thirties, with her natural air of confidence and smart looks, had been in the business for years.

"Well, I don't really know her," said Trevor. "Constance took her on only a few months back. I think she'd seen her in a show at the Almeida or somewhere. Anyway, she's the new kid on Con Covington's books. The less starry amongst us keep plodding away for years and then get to play Buckingham in small-scale tours of *Dickie Three*." Trevor gave a look that said 'that's life' and took a big bite out of his sandwich.

"Oh, don't knock it," I said. "I'm really starting to enjoy it."

Finlay said, "It must have been a bit weird coming here to stage-manage and then getting a part."

"Yes, it was a bit," I admitted. "By the way, I'm loving your music."

"Thanks Brooke," said Finlay. "It's a bit of a case of 'improvise around a theme and hope the boss likes it', but I'm getting there."

Thinking of Finlay's sometimes soulful jazz, sometimes sharply finger-plucked classical, and always captivating guitar playing, I was awestruck. "You're improvising that?"

"Well, yes, kind of," said Finlay. "Jimmy sent me an email about a week ago and told me what he wanted and when he wanted it, but it was all a bit vague. You know, like this afternoon he's doing the scene before Bosworth, when all the ghosts appear to Richard. Jimmy just said he wanted 'something spooky'."

"Well, I suppose that sounds about right," I said.

"Yes," said Finlay, warming to his theme, "but what does that mean musically? I mean, are we talking something along the lines of the theme to *Vertigo*, you know, kind of lush and romantic spooky, or are we thinking more like that film… er… *Halloween*, which is more along the lines of 'There's a psychopath in a funny mask coming to get you'?"

"So what are we getting then?" said Trevor George through a mouthful of sandwich.

"Well, it's more like guitar sound effects than music," said Finlay. "There'll be dissonant chords with apparently random notes. It's kind of vaguely reminiscent of György Ligeti."

"Who's he?" I asked blankly.

"Ever seen *2001: A Space Odyssey*?" asked Finlay.

"Yes, my boyfriend's got it on DVD and I vaguely watched it with him once."

"Right. You know that bit near the beginning when the apes find the obelisk and there's some weird violin music?"

"Yes, I think so." I had a faint memory of apes being mesmerised by this grey obelisk in the desert that emitted a shrill shrieking sound.

"That piece of weird music is by Ligeti. No tune, but very atmospheric," said Finlay.

"And that's what we're getting this afternoon?" asked Trevor George. "Hope Jimmy doesn't have us all leaping around Trevor's throne like monkeys."

Finley laughed. "Hope not. What you're getting this afternoon is inspired by Ligeti rather than nicked from him. I'm just hoping it fits Jimmy's understanding of spooky."

★★★

"Good, very nice, thank you," said Jimmy. "Now let's have a go with the music."

Jimmy's method was to work fairly quickly, getting a very rough shape of the show, so here we were on day four, nearly at the end of the play on a rough blocking; greatly helped by everyone being pretty much off the book on day one. Fortunately for me, it was a play I already knew quite well.

Jimmy's idea for the pre-Bosworth ghost scene was to have Trevor Knightsbridge asleep on his throne, with projections and lighting effects on the screen at the back, and the rest of the cast holding ballroom-type masks and circulating in a direct reference to the party image at the beginning of the play. Also, using plain white ballroom masks made it clear we were ghosts, and also meant that when someone like me, who was playing Lady Anne and also doubling as one of the young princes murdered in the tower, could get away with saying both sets of lines without it being too confusing.

"Come on then pussies, quick as you can please," said Jimmy. "Trevor G, take it from the end of your speech: *sleeping and waking, O defend me still*. That'll give you the timing to pick up your mask. OK. Thank you Finlay, and... off we go!"

Finlay's music brought real flavour to the scene. It was as he'd described: more sound effects than a melody. Having put the idea of prehistoric apes into my head, that, I suppose was my first thought. But it really did sound more like lost souls wailing in the wilderness. Halfway through John Murray's ghost speech as Hastings, Jimmy interrupted.

"Alright thank you. Just pause there a moment. Fin..." Jimmy paused and looked at him thoughtfully. "Yes... bloody good. The only thing is, I know I said spooky, and it is, but if anything it's a little too spooky. I keep expecting Norman Bates to burst up through the trapdoor and start stabbing you all." Jimmy paused again and there was a long silence while he gazed around the room as if trying to catch inspiration from the walls. "I know," he said finally. "We're picking up the idea of the party at the beginning. Trevor K, you know I said that the idea in the opening speech is that everyone's having this fabulous party and you're feeling left out and uninvited and we've got people milling around with drinks in their hands. Well, here we have the polar opposite of that, do you see? This is a party peopled by the ghosts of Richard's past and this time holding white ball-masks. Aaaaaah," he said, as if a lightbulb of inspiration had turned on in his head. "Derek, get hold of some brightly coloured ball masks for that opening scene. I think that would heighten the comparison, do you see?"

While Jimmy had turned to Derek, I caught Trevor George's eye, and he did a quick *2001: A Space Odyssey* ape impersonation in front of the throne while Jimmy's back was turned. I looked at my script to stifle my giggles.

"Now, Fin," said Jimmy, "keep the spooky feel, are you with me? But add some of the jazz feel of that opening scene, so we've got the cross-reference to that; and that'll heighten the idea that Richard's ghosts are actually his memories, do you see?"

"Yes, OK," said Finlay.

"Good... good... yeeeeees, good," said Jimmy. "Let's go again, same place please, thank you Pussy George; thank you Pussy Beckett."

My respect for Finlay and his musical skill went up several notches over the next few minutes. There was the Gershwin-style melody from the opening scene, but in a minor key, with breaks to the rhythm and what I'd started to think of as *2001* bits added. And he could improvise that! As a result of a sudden whim of the director? Astonishing.

"Yes, yes, thank you, that's going to work," Jimmy interrupted again. "Now I'd like to go again, only Trevor K, we need to get you out of that throne. Can't leave you there asleep, do you see? It's not working. As we're going for the party idea, could we get you up and move you downstage, are you with me? Then I think we need to get everyone coming up to you like they're guests at a cocktail party and saying their lines to you, do you see? And everyone, you can even grab his arm to make sure he listens to you, know what I mean? Yes, good. Right, let's go again. Same place please. And… off we go!"

The scene took on a whole new energy. As ghosts of Richard's past, we were grabbing at Trevor like journalists trying to interview a celebrity, except each of us had a message of ill will. I held onto his arm and looked him straight in the eye as the young prince in the tower:

"*Dream on thy cousins smothered in the Tower,*
Let us be lead within thy bosom Richard,
And weigh thee down to ruin, shame and death!
Thy nephews' souls bid thee despair and die!"

Trevor Knightsbridge looked simply terrified. I wasn't sure I liked him, but he was a terrific actor. You could see all the emotion going on behind the eyes.

Next it was John Murray's turn as Hastings. I had four lines to get myself into a different position and adopt the voice and body language of Lady Anne. Then, going up to him like a guest at a party:

"Richard, thy wife, that wretched Anne thy wife,
That never slept a quiet hour with thee,
Now fills thy sleep with perturbations.
Tomorrow in the battle think on me,
And fall thy edgeless sword; despair and die."

In Trevor's eyes was a mixture of regret, remorse and even fear. Brilliant. Great acting. I could see why he got the part.

Next was a speech by Trevor George as Buckingham, and towards the end of this, Jimmy's idea was to have us all in our cocktail party group, behind Richard, half-lit in blue light, and frozen in a tableau for Richard's soliloquy:

"O coward conscience, how dost thou afflict me!
The lights burn blue. It is now dead midnight.
Cold fearful drops stand on my trembling flesh.

My conscience hath a thousand several tongues,
And every tongue brings in a several tale,
And every tale condemns me for a villain.

Methought the souls of all that I had murdered
Came to my tent, and every one did threat
Tomorrow's vengeance on the head of Richard."

Of course there's more to the speech than that, but those were the bits where Jimmy had told Trevor to "Just take in the crowd of ghosts, do you see what I mean? This is where Richard's conscience gets the better of him, and he's as much defeated by the ghosts of his past as he is by Richmond's sword."

So those were the bits I listened out for. Not to give big, upstaging reactions, that would be the worst thing to do, but to get ready to respond to Trevor with a look if it felt right.

It did seem to me that Trevor looked at me more frequently than any of the others, and always with that mixture of regret and fear.

The soliloquy came to an end. Jimmy's idea was for the cocktail party to disperse, for Richard (Trevor) to sit back on his throne and for me to stay where I was; right next to the throne, and as Catesby, to speak the lines telling Richard that it is morning and time to get ready for battle. In the script those lines belong to Ratcliffe, but in Jimmy's version Ratcliffe and Catesby had been amalgamated into one character, played by me. Welcome to the world of small-scale touring.

ME (AS CATESBY): *Nay, good my lord, be not afraid of shadows.*
TREVOR K (AS RICHARD): *By the apostle Paul, shadows tonight*
Have struck more terror to the soul of Richard
Than can the substance of ten thousand soldiers.

And looking into those dark eyes, into the soul of a man who more resembled a frightened child; I believed him.

ARCHIE

Another red-letter day. Sheelagh (Brooke) had come along half an hour before they were due to start, and I'd been standing outside my front door.

Waiting for her.

I tried to tell myself I was just waiting for Old Bill like I usually did, only this time I was waiting outside. I didn't believe myself. I was waiting for Sheelagh as she'd been when I first knew her. Even our conversations had seemed similar to those I'd first had with Sheelagh. Maybe I just wanted to think that. I had to face the fact that soon, Brooke would be gone. Away on tour. But before then would be opening night. And I would be there. That would be a red-letter day to the power of ten.

I did remember her friend Duncan. In a way I wasn't surprised. Spend long enough with theatre people and you realise how small the world is. People know people who know people and so on.

Must get that evening suit out and hope the moths haven't had a go at it.

The main thing I cherished from our talk today was her enthusiasm for the profession. Just like Sheelagh. That infectious, positive energy bubbling away inside that came out in her smile and one could see in her eyes. Her young man, whoever he is, has a firecracker on his hands. Just like I'd had.

OLD BILL

Fido needed to go with her. To be sure. The Young One. Walks fast but he keeps up. Do not let her go through the woods. Make her take the road. The safe way. Away from the bad place.

She gave Fido the slip a day ago, and the day before that. Missed her.

Not today. Fido goes with her to the Warm Drink Man.

BROOKLYN

"Come on Old Bill, I've got to get to work." Somewhere in my head was the thought that I never went through the woods because Old Bill had so clearly told me not to earlier in the week, although I wasn't going to admit that to anyone. It was just too Enid Blyton for words.

Old Bill and I were plodding along Sea Lion Street towards the Institute on a grey morning. Not raining, but looking like it might. It was around nine thirty and as we turned into the small drive leading up to the hall with Archie's house standing dejectedly opposite, Archie was there, by his front door.

"A very good morning my dear, on this somewhat dreary day." He smiled. As soon as he saw Archie, Old Bill went bounding up to him – well, that's an overstatement; he just increased his speed from a slow plod to a slightly faster plod, but his whole body language changed: wagging his tail and his body quivering from side to side.

"I've brought a friend to see you," I said. "Or maybe he brought me, I'm never really sure."

"I'm much in your debt dear lady," said Archie in a touchingly sincere voice, and then looking down at Old Bill, said, "Come on then Fido, time for our usual stroll."

Old Bill wagged his tail and looked so pleased you'd think he'd just been given a marrowbone or something.

"Fido?" I asked.

"Yes, that's just a name I have for him. I'm not sure why, but it seems to fit," chuckled Archie as Old Bill licked his hand.

Oddly enough it did seem to fit. He looked like a Fido, although he also looked like an Old Bill. I laughed. "Well whatever he's called, he's always pleased to see you."

I watched as the two of them walked away through Archie's garden. Even though the black Labrador lived in Beth Churchill's kitchen, I'd come to think of him as Archie's dog. He was an old man who liked to sit and watch the world go by and regularly meet up with a friend and do something they both enjoyed. I realised that that description fitted both Archie and Old Bill, as I watched them disappear into the woods.

Into the woods.

So how come the dog didn't have a problem with Archie going into the woods? His warning me off, earlier this week, had been unmistakeable. Or had it? Who really knew what went on in that doggy mind? Maybe he'd just heard a noise that humans can't hear, or sensed something that humans can't sense.

Whatever. Time to get to work.

***

"Miss McCarthy, a word please."

That was Jimmy's greeting when he arrived that morning. I'd got the kettle on; John, Eleanor, Finley, the two Trevors and Keith were there already, but somehow it still seemed to be my job to make the drinks in the morning. I've always known that the theatre is no place for prima donnas. The best way is to get on with your colleagues and be nice. So I was making the tea as Jimmy came steaming in with his usual energy. *Miss McCarthy*. That didn't sound good.

Silence descended on the rest of the cast. The two Trevors had been chatting about cars, Eleanor and John had been talking about their godchildren, and Finley and Keith had been nominally helping me with the cups, but actually comparing the music of Bernard Hermann with Wagner. Derek followed in Jimmy's wake and without really looking at me, went over to the sound and dimmer desk.

"Sure," I answered, keeping my voice as casual as I could. "Would you like a drink?"

"Yes, the usual please, bring it with you into dressing room one." And with that, he disappeared along the corridor into one of the two rooms which now were used for smaller village hall-type meetings, but in the days of The Hideaway Theatre would have been the dressing rooms.

"Someone got out of bed the wrong side," said Eleanor quietly.

"Yes, well Pussy, I'm very important do you see? Are you with me? Yes, good." Finley's very quiet impersonation at least made me smile.

I carried the boss' tea along the corridor and very nearly knocked on the closed door. Well, he could stuff that. He'd told me to come and see him. And this time I wasn't going to start apologising. If he had a go at me then I would give as good as I got. I walked in, feeling more nervous than I wanted to admit, but determined not to show it. And he'd called me 'Miss McCarthy' in a way I didn't much care for. Well, he could stuff that as well.

He didn't even look at me as I went in. He was standing by the piano, his finger tracing in the dust on the closed lid. As if I was once again just the kid who brought him his tea. Well, sod him.

"Your tea, Mr Knowles."

He looked up and his gaze met mine. There was a long silence as he took the mug of steaming tea and took a sip, his eyes never leaving mine.

I thought that I might have gone too far, but realised that I didn't much care if I had. In that moment I discovered that actually I was far less afraid of this man than I'd thought. Yes, he was my boss, and yes, he had given me my first break, but that didn't mean I had to let him use me as a doormat. In my mind were Duncan's words about Archie: *He was the real thing. Genuine old school. Jimmy's more of a modern imitation. Like a mock antique.*

"You still make a good cup of tea," said Jimmy. "By the way, where's yours?"

In my nervous fluster, I'd left my morning coffee on the draining board. "Back in the kitchen," I said.

"Well, go and get it, and come back."

When I appeared back in the kitchen the others all looked at me expectantly. They had clearly been talking about what had happened. Seven curious pairs of eyes were on me. I just shrugged, picked up my coffee and went back to the dressing room.

"Take a seat," said Jimmy, who by this time was sitting on the piano stool.

I sat down on the chair beside the piano.

"Well, Brooksy, I'm a little disappointed."

Right. Sod him and stuff him. "Well I'm sorry Jimmy, but I really don't know what you want me to do differently. I'm playing a set of parts I only found out I was playing three days ago. Fortunately for both of us, I already knew the Lady Anne part pretty well anyway, and as for Catesby and the young prince, I've been cramming that in every break and every evening, and so far I've managed most of the time on stage without a script. You haven't given much by way of specific direction, and I know that's because you've worked quickly to get a general shape of the play, so if I've disappointed you I'm sorry…"

I could feel my voice starting to crack as I let out this pent-up emotion. Fighting to regain control I said, "And one other thing: my name is Brooke. Or Brooklyn. Please don't call me Miss McCarthy in the way you did just then, and never under any circumstances expect me to answer if you call me Pussy!"

Jimmy Knowles just stared at me. He took another sip at his tea. I pulled out a handkerchief, partly for something to do in the icy silence, partly to dry my eyes which had started to water, and partly because after my final comment I actually wanted to laugh. It was one of those lines said in anger in a comedy, which brings the house down in the theatre.

"Well… Brooklyn," said Jimmy gravely. "I do hope that's got whatever it was out of your system. Come on, dry your eyes, no need for waterworks. Have some coffee."

When I next looked at him he actually smiled in a thin sort of way. "Note to self: explain more clearly," he said. "What I meant was that I was disappointed that you hadn't spoken to me about your contract and this BBC job of yours."

"Oh, I see. Yes, well I was going to, but my agent said it was better if he handled that."

"Did he now?" said Jimmy. "'Course he did, cheeky bugger. Probably makes him feel important in his Covent Garden bedsit or whatever he calls his office. I don't like agents. It's the actors I work with, so if they're not happy, they can bloody well talk to me. Understood?"

"OK, fair comment, but I'm with an agent. That means you talk to him about money. That's his job."

Another silence. I could feel this conversation threatening to turn into an argument.

"Alright Brooke, I'll give you that. I didn't much like the little prick, but he's got you an extra forty quid a week, so I hope you're happy, and the opening night drinks are on you." Jimmy gave a bleak smile.

Forty pounds a week extra. *Thank you Crispin.* No wonder Jimmy didn't like agents.

"Another thing I don't like about agents," Jimmy continued; "they think they're God. Think they can just pull actors out of a project when a better offer comes along. Had a dose of that earlier this week. Con bloody Covington suddenly phoning up and cancelling Rachel Powell's contract like that. Bugger all I could do about it because the little cow hadn't actually signed on the dotted line. I bet that was Con's idea as well. Scheming bitch. She might have some big film contacts but that's no excuse. And that Rachel only appeared on the scene two years ago. God knows where she was before then, but I'll tell you something for nothing, she won't work in my theatre again, and the theatre's a small world." Jimmy took another sip at his tea. "Anyway, at least this Crispin man of yours didn't do that. And at least this *Crimewatch* thing is on one of the days off."

"Yes, well, like I say, I was going to tell you."

Jimmy waved his hand dismissively. "I know, talk to my agent." He paused. "Brooklyn, let me give you some advice."

Now what was coming? Another sermon on Jimmy's view of the theatrical world and my part in it? Advice on characterisation that ran counter to everything I'd learned at college?

"Agents aren't the be-all and end-all, you know. They work for you, not the other way round. Rachel what's-her-name will find that out to her cost if she hasn't already. And… now listen carefully Brooke." Jimmy Knowles leant closer to me and looked me straight in the eyes. "It's a well-known fact that compliments from me are about as common as heat waves in the Arctic, and you may not get another if you work for me every season between now and Doomsday." He paused to make sure I was listening, then he went on. "You're more than twice the actress she is. When you read in for her you were so clearly the obvious choice for the role that I don't know why I hadn't seen it before." Jimmy reached into his briefcase. "So here you are Brooklyn. New contract typed up by the Lady Gemma this morning. New rate of pay, new statement saying we're happy for you to work for the Beeb on your day off. Now just sign the bloody thing, then I'll know I've got you for the show, and we can get on with some work."

***

My interview with Jimmy had taken about twenty minutes. When we came back in, no doubt with me grinning like a Halloween mask, the worried faces relaxed a bit and were replaced by a nonchalant curiosity, with an eager expectation of finding out the gossip later.

"Right then you lazy buffoons, time to do some work," said Jimmy in his grumpiest voice. "Just working sections this morning, starting with the scene where Hastings gets his death sentence, and then this afternoon we'll have a stagger through the whole thing and we'll see where we are, where the holes are, and therefore what you need to think about over the weekend. By this time next week the whole thing needs to be as tight as a thumbscrew and as smooth as a symphony."

Old school. Jimmy's style of speech hovered somewhere between theatrical camp and military disciplinarian. He was as likely to call you Pussy as he was to call you a lazy bastard. He had some genuinely good instincts about the theatre, seemed to like actors, yet employed this 'my way or the highway' tone with everyone who worked with him. Yet people came back for more. Eleanor had clearly worked with him many times. As had Keith. And Derek. Trevor Knightsbridge had worked with him at least once before. All of that said something positive.

And now he had paid me a huge compliment. *More than twice the actress she is.* Only a few days after he had said something along the lines of "We're getting the real actress back tomorrow", when referring to Rachel Powell, whom I had thought seemed very good when I'd watched her on day one. So very long ago.

***

At lunchtime Jimmy and Derek disappeared over the road to the pub while the rest of us sat around with plastic pots of pasta salad (Finlay), bread rolls and chorizo (Keith), Ryvita, cheese and lettuce (Eleanor), an enormous submarine salad roll (John), a bowl of cereal (Trevor George), a pack of sandwiches and some fruit bought from Bateman's (Trevor Knightsbridge and me).

The conversation, of course, was what the boss had wanted to see me for. I played down the compliments by telling the others something to the effect that Jimmy was pleased with what I was doing and was just concerned I wasn't taking on too much by agreeing to do the *Crimewatch* job. The congratulation was muted about that, and I could understand why.

"Apparently I look a bit like the murdered girl," I said.

"You do," said Trevor Knightsbridge abruptly.

"Bloody hell Trev," said Trevor George after a couple of seconds of tangible silence, "don't freak her out."

"Sorry. It's just… she does," said Trevor Knightsbridge, looking down again.

"No it's fine," I said. "I suppose if the Old Bill find the killer then I'll have done some good." Only once the words were out did I realise I'd used the cockney slang for the police. The Old Bill. The same name as Beth's dog. Or not, according to Archie.

"Terrible thing," said Finlay, "and in the woods just here."

"Well no, not quite," said Eleanor a little sharply. "To hear people talk you'd think the poor girl was murdered only a hundred yards from here, and that there's a killer behind every tree."

"So where was it?" I asked, imagining Scott telling me again to watch the news more often than I did.

"About two miles away," said Eleanor. "Forgers Wood lies between here and Dunslinton village. There's a long, meandering footpath that gets used by dog walkers and joggers. You can get to it from the Port St Catherine Road on the one side and any number of smaller roads between here and Dunslinton. She was found about a hundred yards away from that footpath on the Port St Catherine side. The papers needed the name of the nearest town and decided Cranton Oh was it."

"I thought it was just behind the Institute," I said, remembering Beth's warning on the first day."

"'Course you did," said Eleanor, "it's called gossip. Something dreadful happens and people like to make it sound even worse. Makes me sick. Saying you live near where a murder took place is in the same league as getting a kick out of visiting the site of a disaster."

"Don't walk through the woods," said Keith, attempting to lighten the mood.

"Not likely," I said, and took a bite of sandwich.

***

The run-through in the afternoon did precisely what Jimmy said it would do: show up the holes. My Lady Anne scenes went quite well; the sticky points for me were the Catesby scenes and the scene as the young prince. Somehow when we'd rehearsed that scene, we'd got sidetracked into talking about music. Finley was playing the elder of the two princes, but at the start of the scene had been playing regal music on his guitar. So that rehearsal had devolved into a discussion of where the music would start and stop and where Finlay's very expensive guitar would be put while he was being the prince. So that scene felt like a read-through.

I did like Jimmy's idea of the cocktail party at the opening being recalled in the ghost scene though. Also, he had borrowed an idea from the Ian McKellen film, and had inserted some of Richard's lines from *HenryVI Part Three* into the opening speech:

Why, I can smile, and murder while I smile;
And cry content to that which grieves my heart;
And wet my cheeks with artificial tears
And frame my face to all occasions.

Then back into:

Plots have I laid, inductions dangerous,
By drunken prophecies, libels and dreams,
To set my brother Clarence and the King
In deadly hate the one against the other.

This was effectively our cue to disperse the cocktail party scene, and for Finlay and Keith to get ready to reappear as Clarence and Brackenbury.

At the end of the rehearsal Jimmy gave a few specific notes

and then signed off with: "But it wasn't bad, pussies all, not bad at all. Wouldn't yet part up with my hard-earned cash to see it, but we've got another week till we open, and at the start of next week we'll have the frocks, so have a good weekend, don't drink the bars dry, and get here on Monday at ten, bright-eyed and bushy-tailed. Thank you all very much."

And with that, he let us go and started talking to Derek about the lighting plot.

As I walked back past Archie's cottage I did look to see if he was around, but no lights were on. Probably asleep.

What would I do tonight? The truth was that I still felt like a bit of an outsider. Suddenly I felt alone in a strange place with no one to go out for a drink with. The others were all nice enough, but they had their own lives to lead. The people I felt the most comfortable with were Eleanor, who was going home to her husband, and Finlay; but he and his partner were going out for a meal. Ironically, Rachel, whose part I was now playing, was the only other one with whom I felt I had anything in common.

I walked back to my digs and ended up sharing a wonderful homemade shepherds' pie with Beth. Old Bill was watching us, probably in the hope of some titbits.

The conversation, of course, was the play and how it was going. Beth was excited by the drama of my getting a 'proper part' as opposed to 'just' stage-managing. I managed to keep the conversation away from *Crimewatch* though. I still felt a bit odd about it, and didn't need any more stories about murderers lurking in the woods.

With a big glass of Beth's red wine, I went up to my room, opened up my laptop and spent the next hour or so surfing the net. First I checked my emails. In amongst the usual junk from Amazon special offers and spam from people trying to sell me replica wristwatches was one from Crispin:

Hi Brooke,

Attached copy of your contract for Crimewatch which I've signed on your behalf; also a call sheet and script.

Best,

Cx

I opened it up. The schedule was very straightforward. I was called for six in the evening, at the Pelican Club in Port St Catherine. There was a room there set aside for the crew. We had an hour for costume and make up, then at seven we would start the shoot. Lynn Arthur had left the bar where she worked at nine thirty and had been seen on the town's CCTV cameras walking away from the Seafront. There would be a few shots of me, as Lynn, serving customers in the bar, then of me leaving the bar and walking along the road away from the Seafront. Then a scene on the footpath in the woods where she was found. *Yeah, I know: don't walk through the woods. Relax; there'll be a whole film crew with me to guard against the psychos.* Attached were some photographs of Lynn. I had to admit she did look like me: same petite build, elfin face. Similar hairstyle, although whereas I had a fringe, hers was parted to one side; apart from that we could almost be sisters.

I surfed onto Facebook. I'm not a great one for constantly updating my status, but I did put: *First week done, only a week till we open and feeling great to be playing a proper part. #Richard3* That would hopefully get some 'likes' and comments to help with my feeling of loneliness.

I scrolled down the home page. The usual mix of interesting stuff from genuine friends, invitations to 'like' pages to do with productions some of my mates are involved with, as well as stuff I really can't be bothered with such as 'Which character from *Game of Thrones* are you?'

"Chance would be a fine thing," I said aloud, and thought to myself that Crispin probably didn't have contacts quite that good.

Just then the little icon at the top of the screen came on. *Trevor Knightsbridge likes your status.* Trevor. I'd forgotten I'd accepted his friend request. I was about to have a look at his profile page when the icon flashed again: *Rachel Powell commented on your status.*

Rachel. Only then did I notice that the 'friends' icon also had a *1* illuminated: *Rachel Powell accepted your friend request.* I followed the link and Rachel had written: *Glad it worked out for you. Don't feel so bad about dropping you in it now.* ☺

I 'liked' her comment and wrote: *Thanks Rachel. It's a bit bunny-in-headlights at times, but going OK. Hope your plans work out. Bx*

That seemed the end of the conversation. The easy familiarity with someone I quite liked, but really didn't actually know at all.

From there to someone I admired, but wasn't sure whether I liked. Trevor Knightsbridge. His profile picture was clearly also his Spotlight photo. In black and white; a moody, intense stare which probably worked quite well for acting jobs but wasn't really suitable for the humorous, casual world of Facebook. A few status updates. One from the start of the week: *Check out the Edwardian Palace Richard III tour. Starts in a fortnight. Yours truly as Dick the Shit.*

Scrolling further down, most of the updates were, in effect, information and photographs to do with Trevor's latest job. Very interesting if you fancied seeing him act, but no sense of fun. I mean, like, what did the guy think about stuff? What did he like? I was reaching the conclusion that what Trevor liked best, was Trevor.

I was about to surf away, when for some reason I stopped at a photograph. Maybe it was because in it, Trevor Knightsbridge was smiling happily. Not at all like the man I'd grown accustomed to. The photograph had been taken on a night out. In fact it was probably a 'selfie' taken by the girl Trevor had his arm around. The girl who looked just like me. The girl whose picture I had just been looking at in my *Crimewatch* script.

Lynn Arthur.

I don't know how long I looked at the picture. Maybe seconds, maybe minutes. There was no name tag that appeared when I hovered the cursor over her image, but it was definitely Lynn. So Trevor had known her. How? In the picture they looked like they were an item. A happy, 'this is us having a good time' couple shot. Was I reading too much into it? Lynn Arthur must have known many people before she became a murder victim. Trevor was one of them.

The way Trevor had looked at me.

And sometimes had avoided looking at me. The strong emotions he'd been showing in the Lady Anne and Richard scene, which I'd just put down to his fine acting. Was it because when he looked at me, he saw her?

Then after we'd finished the scene he'd paid me a compliment: I'd thought it odd at the time, but hadn't said anything. Not the compliment, but what seemed to be just a new abbreviation of my name. Well, I didn't want to seem like a diva. He'd said that he thought I did great. Which was nice. Except he'd used the wrong name. What he actually said was "Lynn, just to say I thought you did great."

Lynn.

I scrolled further down his profile page looking for other photos of her. None at all. The one of Trevor and Lynn was the only truly personal photograph in Trevor's profile.

Suddenly there was a timid knock on my door. "Brooke?" It was Beth.

"Yes, come in," I said, looking up as Beth appeared.

"You've got a visitor," she said.

My first thought, completely irrationally, was that this was going to be Trevor Knightsbridge. I must have looked startled.

"It's alright, nothing to worry about," said Beth, standing to one side and opening the door further. A good-looking man in his twenties with blond hair walked in.

Scott.

***

I woke up wondering where I was. Then turned over and found Scott beside me. We were in a hotel in Bournemouth for the weekend. Scott's arrival had been so wonderfully unexpected that I'd burst into tears as I hugged him.

He'd said, "No, Brooklyn, me coming here was supposed to cheer you up, not make you cry."

I giggled with tears rolling down my cheeks.

Then we'd gone out for dinner in an Indian restaurant. Scott had a balti and I just had a starter of tandoori chicken – all I could manage after Beth's shepherd's pie.

"I wish you'd told me you were coming," I said.

"But that would have spoilt the surprise. Anyway, it wasn't planned for very long. Really only yesterday evening when Pete asked me when I'd be seeing you next." Pete was one of Scott's work colleagues who he sometimes went for a drink with after work. "That made me think; you know what? If I've got an actress for a girlfriend, I'd better get used to travelling around the country seeing stuff. So I booked the hotel, got in the car, and here I am."

The hotel was at the top of the cliffs overlooking the bay. The weather's a bit bracing at the end of February. We stayed in bed till about ten, had a leisurely breakfast, went for a walk into the town and along the beach, and just generally relaxed like anybody else on a holiday weekend.

There was one unspoken thought which whined away in my mind, a bit like when you hear a mosquito buzzing in your bedroom once you've turned out the light. You hear it in the silence, and it won't go away: *Crimewatch*, Lynn Arthur and Trevor Knightsbridge. Eventually I just had to say something as we were walking along the promenade.

"Scott… look, you know that *Crimewatch* job? Well it's come through and I've said I'll do it."

"Yes, I thought so," said Scott.

"You thought so?"

"Yes… well, it's work I suppose. It's what you do. And it beats the hell out of temping at Baxter Kendrick."

"Yes, true. There's not much to it anyway. Just a few shots in the bar then walking down the road."

Scott smiled wanly. "Well, I suppose it's not as if you're having to do a bedroom scene with some other guy."

I thumped him playfully on the shoulder and laughed.

"It's just…" He paused, searching for the phrase. "You know, with you living down here and being such a close match with what's-her-name, Lynn Arthur, it just feels a bit like… well…"

I finished the sentence for him. "Tempting fate."

After that there was nothing else to say.

***

I was glad I'd had that conversation with Scott. The *Crimewatch* job felt more like an ominous cloud on the horizon than an exciting offer of work, and part of me even wished it hadn't come my way. Then I told myself I was being silly. *Get a grip on yourself girl; you only got the job because of the way you look. That's just as true of Crimewatch as it would be if you got a part as a Bond girl. It's looks. Not talent.*

I did decide against telling Scott about the Trevor Knightsbridge connection though. I knew him well enough to know that he would think it was too much of a coincidence. Tempting fate. With Scott feeling uneasy about the *Crimewatch* job, I didn't want him also worrying about someone I worked with.

OK, so Trevor had known Lynn. So what? It might mean he'd had a relationship with her. It explained the odd looks he had given me in rehearsal, and how he had sometimes avoided my eyes. It meant nothing beyond that.

But the whining of the worry-mosquito didn't stop.

***

Sunday night. Back in my room at Beth's. We'd checked out of the hotel room at twelve, went for a coffee, then for a walk. It was a cold drizzly day and we huddled together under an umbrella as we walked, but after about half an hour got into Scott's BMW and drove round the coast to Port St Catherine and had a traditional Sunday roast in a pub.

After that, with our weekend nearly over and with the rain getting heavier, we decided to head back to Beth's where we sat on the bed and watched episodes of *Friends* on my laptop.

Then at about six, we said our goodbyes. Well, you know

how that one goes by now. I watched from under the umbrella as Scott's car disappeared along the Port St Catherine road. Then I went up to my room, which still held the presence of the man I loved.

I sat back on the bed and looked glumly at Mr Tibbs as I had first done exactly a week ago. *Right. Glass of wine. Stop feeling sorry for yourself and do some work.*

I wonder if directors know that when they tell you to have a think about something over the weekend, very often the first thought you give it is last thing on a Sunday night. The weekend with Scott had been wonderful. I'd been able to switch off completely from the job and relax. There was something very old-fashioned and gentlemanly about Scott. He hadn't said as much, but somewhere among his reasons for coming down to see me for a surprise visit was the idea of wanting to protect me. In his own way he'd whisked me away to a fortress to look after me. The hotel on the cliffs had even looked a bit like a fairytale castle with a tall turret. *Rapunzel, Rapunzel, let down your hair.*

Anyway. Work. First do those lines I made such a mess of in the Princes scene, where the young Prince Edward, (me) later to be murdered at Richard's orders, has arrived in London and is 'advised' by his Uncle Richard that he will be happiest and safest in the Tower of London:

ME: *I do not like the Tower, of any place.*
Did Julius Caesar build that place, my lord?
BUCKINGHAM: *He did, my gracious lord, begin that place.*
ME: *But say, my lord, it were not registered, Methinks the truth should live from age to age.*
RICHARD (aside): *So wise so young, they say, do never live long.*

I went over the scene several times before I was happy. It's easy enough to know your lines in your bedroom, but once you get the scene on its feet you always find out how well you really know them.

I worked until about nine, got through two large glasses of red wine and had some of Beth's gloriously sinful homemade flapjack. Idly, I flicked through the script; the opening cocktail party. I could even hear Finlay's music in my head. The Lady Anne scene, the 'blue lighting' scene before the Battle of Bosworth where Richard is confronted by his memories and Finlay plays his mix of jazz and weird science fiction-classic music.

Confronted by memories: Richard's ghosts as clear and real to him as was the presence of Scott in this room after I'd said goodbye and seen him on his way back to London. Richard's past deeds, which earlier in the play he had celebrated, come back to haunt him before the battle which ends in his death.

Too much red wine. I felt a bit lightheaded as I got into bed, and the combination of rich food and booze meant that I didn't sleep properly till gone two. Trying to sleep, I'd ended up checking Facebook and Twitter. Then, unwisely, I looked again at Trevor Knightsbridge's profile and the girl I would be playing in just over a week's time. The girl who now only existed in photographs and memories. The picture itself a representation of a memory, by all appearances a happy one with two smiling faces.

Maybe it was the effect of the red wine and feeling overtired, but the line from the play that wouldn't leave my head was the one Jimmy had given to Trevor to include in the opening speech:

I can smile, and murder while I smile.

***

"Tell me why I don't like Mondays," I mumbled to myself as I looked at my pale, shell-shocked face in the mirror.

I had slept eventually. Probably more than I thought. With a sleepless night, the bits you remember are those bits where you lie awake. I remember checking the time at 1.50, and I reckon I was still awake an hour later, but didn't really know.

An ice-cold shower to wake me up, and a paracetamol to get rid of the nagging headache had me feeling more human by the time I left for work, later than usual at 9.40. *Right. Sod it. The shortcut through the woods. It's not 'tempting fate', it's not haunted; it's not even near where Lynn Arthur was found. It's just a shortcut and that's all. It's also a bright, clear morning and not the middle of the night.*

Old Bill was walking ahead of me and I'm ashamed to admit I dodged around behind him so I was walking down the path before he noticed. He gave a woof of indignant protest. *Really?* I wasn't in the best frame of mind to be honest, but even so, I felt a pang of conscience.

"Come on then Fido," I said, using Archie's name for him. "I'm late and if you're with me I'll be OK."

Old Bill stopped, cocked his head on one side as though he understood, wagged his tail and his whole body seemed to shake with pleasure. Daft old dog.

"Come on then if you're coming," I said, slapping my hand against my thigh, encouraging him to come with me.

The old black Labrador and I walked along what in fact was a gravelled cycle path complete with *Cyclists please give way to pedestrians* signs and those little bins for bags of dogshit. "Don't get any funny ideas Fido," I said; "that's Beth's job, or Archie's if you ask nicely. You're just someone I walk to work with."

Old Bill looked up at me, and if he'd been human I think he would have winked.

The cycle path, from where I joined it to the point I would leave it at the small gap behind the Institute, would be about a quarter of a mile, tops. Other paths led away from it, deeper into the woods, presumably some of them leading to where Lynn had been found. No way was I going down any of those.

Suddenly I heard a noise just behind me. The sound of someone running through leaves and twigs. I turned. Trevor Knightsbridge, dressed in running shorts and a baseball cap, his mouth drawn into a snarl, was coming towards me fast.

My arms flew up in defence. I nearly dropped my bag. I remember hearing myself give a girly gasp of shock.

"Sorry love, didn't mean to scare you," said the man, panting and smiling. "You OK?" He wasn't Trevor, and didn't even look much like him. He was just an ordinary guy out for a morning run.

"Yes, sorry." I laughed weakly. "Just startled me that's all."

"All the best, love." He gave a friendly wave and ran off farther along the path.

What was the matter with me? It wasn't until I arrived at the hall that I felt calm again. Archie was waiting outside his front door. Old Bill went towards him wagging his tail.

"I'll talk to you later." I smiled apologetically to Archie and went inside.

Coming to work through the woods was not a good idea, I decided. I might have saved a little time, but I hadn't called at Bateman's and bought my lunchtime sandwiches, and I'd been scared half to death by a morning runner. Maybe my older, wiser, four-legged friend really did know things I didn't.

Fido realised the Young One knew his name as well. The Warm Drink Man and the Young One knew things no one else did. They knew his name. But how, Fido didn't know.

The Young One went through the woods. Not near where the Bad Thing happened. But near enough. Fido was glad he went with her. The Quick Panting Man he sometimes saw running scared her. Really scared her. She didn't need to be. That man didn't have the Cain Scent. But the Young One had been scared. Fido had smelled the Craven Scent.

Not sure why she'd been scared. The Quick Panting Man was running like he always did. Smiling; share-thinking with the Young One. He never did that when Fido walked with the Warm Drink Man. But then the Warm Drink Man was never scared. So the Quick Panting Man didn't need to make share-thinking noises.

Maybe the Young One knew things Fido didn't.

BROOKLYN

With only five days' rehearsal left until we opened, Jimmy was not suffering fools gladly, and worked fast. As my dad would say, he was taking no prisoners. If he thought something was crap then he'd say so as bluntly as he had to me earlier in the week. Although he was in his sixties he had tremendous drive and energy and was what some would describe as a force of nature. Duncan had told me how much Jimmy had admired the man who was his predecessor: Archie Stephens. Maybe some of Archie's energy had transferred itself to Jimmy. Or maybe it's just the theatre and constant creative energy that keeps people young. Either way, I hope that when I'm sixty I have as much energy as Jimmy but nicer manners, and if I get to be ninety-eight I hope I have the same lively spark as Archie.

At lunchtime I had to walk back in the direction of my digs to Bateman's grocery shop. The others had brought their usual lunchtime fare. Even Jimmy had a sandwich box and a flask and announced, "Now then pussies all, just forty minutes nosebag time today. Then back to the grindstone."

So I grabbed my purse from my bag and went as quickly as I could. Maybe five minutes there, five minutes back, and thirty minutes to eat. Should be enough.

As I got to the door, Trevor Knightsbridge appeared beside me. "Going to the shop?"

"Er yes," I said, already looking for an escape route. "Can I get you anything?"

"No, its fine, I'll come with you." The dark eyes met mine.

"Yeah, sure," I said, trying to sound like I didn't mind one way or the other. I couldn't even use Archie as an excuse for Trevor to go on without me. Archie was nowhere to be seen either in his garden or through the murky windows of his house. Trevor and I walked in glum silence to the road and turned left towards the shop.

"Good weekend?" he asked.

"Yes, lovely thanks. Did you?"

"Yeah… it was OK. Yeah, all good. So what did you do?"

"Well, my boyfriend, Scott, came down and took me away for the weekend to Bournemouth. All very romantic…" I trailed off. "You?"

"Nothing much. Did some work. Big fucker of a part to get to grips with. Stayed at home mostly."

"And where is home?"

"I've got a little place by the New Forest. It's handy for London when I need to get there. But also good for work down here."

Another silence; broken by Trevor. "So you saw the photograph then?"

For an instant I had no idea what he meant. "The photograph?"

"Of Lynn and me. On my Facebook page." The dark eyes looked at me.

There was no point in denying it, but still I felt like I'd been caught doing something I shouldn't. "Yes, I saw it," I said simply.

"She was a lovely girl," said Trevor, staring ahead.

I couldn't think of anything to say but still blurted out, "So… did you know her well?"

"Well, what do you think?" he said a little darkly.

This past week I'd had a gutful of being intimidated by older, more forceful personalities than my own, and things were going to change.

"I think that every time you look at me you think of her, and that's why you've been so off with me ever since we met," I said.

He said nothing. Just looked at me and nodded briefly. "Yeah, sorry about that. You're so like her, you have no idea."

Sod this. I wasn't going to be made to feel bad just because I happened to remind him of his dead girlfriend. "You just need to remember that I'm me and not her," I said, trying to be gentle but not, you know, feeling it. "Right. Now we've cleared the air about this I'm going to have a BLT, you're going to have whatever you're having, and then we're going to get on with the job and say no more about it. Got it?"

We walked back in silence.

***

The next few days were intense, full-on days. On Tuesday we spent the morning mixing and matching costumes, with Jimmy impatiently wanting to "get the frocks sorted once and for all, and get on with rehearsing".

Wednesday was, in effect, our second dress rehearsal, and then Jimmy worked on bits of the play that hadn't gone as planned. Thursday was a cue-to-cue technical run mostly for Derek and Keith's benefit, and Friday was another dress rehearsal. Trevor Knightsbridge and I behaved professionally towards each other and seemed to get on OK, but I could still see in his eyes the trace of our conversation on the way to get our lunchtime sandwiches. It did cross my mind to apologise for perhaps speaking a bit harshly, but I resisted that thought. I'd done too much apologising on this job already.

My mornings had taken on a regular pattern. Leave Beth's house at about half nine and take a slower walk than I would normally, with Old Bill plodding beside me along Sea Lion Street. My one trip into the woods earlier in the week had put me off going that way again. Archie would either be waiting for us, or would appear through the door, which always seemed to be open an inch or two, probably so he could hear us arrive.

On the Saturday morning I was there a little earlier. Only by about five minutes, but sure enough, there was Archie, only this time in full evening dress, at nine twenty-five in the morning.

"Hello," I said, "was it a good party?"

Archie looked confused and I instantly regretted my rather unfunny joke. "What's that my dear?"

Old Bill greeted Archie as he usually did, by wiggling his body and wagging his tail. He sniffed at Archie's trousers, and then gave a big doggy sneeze. Probably the smell of mothballs, of which I'd also just caught a whiff.

"Nothing, it's just you look like you've been to a party," I said and then, clumsy, insensitive klutz that I am, I added, "I wondered if you'd been up all night."

Archie gave one of his little wistful smiles. "No, dear lady. No party I'm afraid. And as for being up all night, well, sometimes I wonder if I have been. When you get to – what was it? – ah yes, ninety-eight, dear me, ninety-eight, for some reason you don't seem to need so much sleep. I've just dug out the old suit for the show tonight. Haven't worn this since… well… since the Hideaway days. Thought I'd get rid of the mothball smell if I wore it today."

I smiled. He was such a sweetie that I didn't want to risk hurting him by laughing. Apparently we had thirty tickets pre-sold for the opening show that night, I guess mostly to locals, but I bet there weren't many so excited that they were trying out their glad rags this early in the morning.

"I say, my dear. Could you tell me how much the tickets are?" said Archie.

I realised that I had no idea. "Sorry, no, I don't know. I'm guessing a tenner or so. Personally I think they should let you in for free with your history here."

"No, no my dear. I'll pay my dues. Ten pounds though. Dear me. Back in the early days here it was only a shilling. Nowadays I don't suppose that would even buy you a programme." He gave another of his wistful smiles. "Ah well... until tonight, young Brooke." Like when we'd first met, I half-expected him to kiss my hand. Maybe it was the formal evening clothes that heightened the old-world charm that he naturally had. "Come along then Fido," he said, and he and Old Bill walked away, Archie with his smooth, gliding stroll, Fido with his purposeful plod. I stood and watched them go, two old friends off for their daily walk. I found myself wondering how far they went and how long they took. And whether anyone else would notice that Archie was dressed like a 1930s newsreader and would think it strange.

★★★

After watching Archie and Fido disappear into the woods, I stood for a minute or two just enjoying the morning, and feeling glad I was actually doing the job I had trained for. OK, so it was 'only' a small-scale tour. But it was proper theatre, and I was loving it. Meeting Archie, the classic old theatrical, was the icing on the cake.

To my surprise, I'd also grown quite fond of Jimmy. He didn't suffer fools gladly, and his habit of calling people 'Pussy' was rude, irritating and inappropriate. But give the guy his due; he got results. You knew where you were with him, and provided you turned up on time, knew your lines and didn't waste time, then the sarcastic comments became fewer and occasionally you'd even get a "Yes... good. Bloody good. No need to go back over that."

First item on the day's schedule was a post mortem on yesterday's dress run. Jimmy's verdict was along the lines of: "Not bad. In fact certain sections are getting closer to what I might not begrudge a tenner to see."

He spent nearly an hour giving notes on what he called "tweaks and nudges". A few for me, many to do with timing of costume changes, and then he said, "Now... what's this? Ah yes, Brooklyn..." He paused for a few moments and looked upwards. Then he said:

"*When he that is my husband now*

Came to me as I followed Henry's corse... – that speech. Try to pull apart the text a bit. Play the contrast, do you see?"

My face must have said that I didn't.

"*He that is my husband now...*" repeated Jimmy, and indicated Trevor Knightsbridge. "In other words this foul devil, murderer and everything you hate and fear. Then you talk about your other angel husband: *and that dear saint which then I weeping followed* – we need to sense the contrast more, do you see? Play the contrast Brooklyn. Your dearest love has been murdered by your worst nightmare, who is now your husband. Tell me Brooklyn, do you have a boyfriend?"

"Er... yes, Scott," I replied, wondering as I said it why I named him.

Jimmy went on: "Right-oh, just think of this: the lovely Trevor here has murdered Scott and then married you, and what's more, you know that he hates you and one day soon will murder you. Go with that thought process and see what happens, are you with me? That's what I need to believe in order for that speech to work. Do you see?"

"Yeah sure, OK," I said, and Jimmy went on to the next item on his list. It had been a very constructive note, but all the same I felt a little crestfallen. I'd been using that thought process from the start. At college my training had been very much based on using your own experience to feed what you do as an actor. OK Jimmy, fair comment, I'm on the right lines, just use the text and ramp up the contrast.

Besides, he hates me and will no doubt shortly be rid of me. Since my conversation with Trevor Knightsbridge a few days previously, that line has become much easier to deliver.

***

Half past six, and we finished the final notes session after the dress run.

Jimmy had made us do a speed run after the morning notes. I hate speed runs. You go through the entire play speaking every line as quickly as possible, any moves done at a run, and all pauses eliminated. It's useful for showing up any weak points but that's about it. Afterwards I felt like my brain had been fried, and I was more in need of a double gin than yet another rehearsal.

But another rehearsal was what we had. "There is no such thing as being over-rehearsed," Jimmy said emphatically. "You can feel over-rehearsed, but you're not. Are you with me? The way out of feeling over-rehearsed is actually more rehearsal, do you see? That way you can tease out all that wonderful detail that lies hidden in the text."

He was right of course, but I was still fed up that we'd only get an hour between the end of the dress and the half.

Beth Churchill and a few others were busying around the hall arranging chairs and preparing wine glasses and boxes of wine on a table at the back of the hall. A man I guessed was in his early seventies seemed to be the one in charge, and I went and said hello to him, largely, I suppose, to keep things sweet with the locals who were selling our tickets.

"Hello, I'm Brooke, playing Lady Anne."

"Pleased to meet you, I'm Martin. Martin Helgin."

"Oh, so you're the mysterious keyholder," I said perhaps a little untactfully. "I saw your name on the sign outside."

"Yes, I keep a low profile." He smiled. "Quite a good house tonight and I think we'll get a decent walk-up from people in the village. Anybody with a bit more taste than to watch *The X Factor* anyway."

"Well, we'll do our best to be better than that," I said.

"This is a new venture for us," said Martin. "The committee were quite keen on the idea to get a professional show here again. To see if Jimmy Knowles has the Stephens factor in putting this place back on the map."

"Amazing guy," I said.

"Yes, he's been very impressive running the Palace Theatre, so we'll see how this touring idea of his works here."

I was about to say that the 'amazing guy' I meant was Archie Stephens, when I saw him standing in the lobby.

"Excuse me a minute," I said to Martin and went over to Archie in the lobby. I was as excited to see him as if I were a child at boarding school whose grandfather had turned up to see a school play, but as I said hello to him I kept my voice low. Something in me told me that this very old-school theatrical might take the view that I shouldn't really be talking to the public till after the show.

"Good evening Brooke my dear, will I do?" He indicated his evening suit. "I hope I don't smell too much of mothballs."

"Yes, you'll do," I said in the same way that my mum used to say when she was packing me off to school. The smell of mothballs was quite strong, but somehow that added to Archie's antique theatrical charm.

"I suppose I shouldn't be here just yet," said Archie, "but I'm so looking forward to it that I just couldn't keep away." The piercing eyes practically sparkled with excitement.

I giggled. "I was just talking about you with Martin over there." I indicated Martin Helgin, who was shaking hands with Derek and Trevor Knightsbridge. Trevor stared at me strangely. *Just being Trevor I guess.*

"Really my dear? How splendid," said Archie. "I must go and have a chat with him, but I don't want to get in the way."

"I'm sure he'd love to see you. In fact he was singing your praises. Hoping this show has what he called 'the Stephens factor'."

"I am much indebted to him," said Archie.

"I should go," I said. "I need to relax and have a quick bite to eat before we start."

"Quite so my dear. In plenty of time for the half. Enjoy the show."

"Do hang around afterwards. I'd love to introduce you to Scott."

"Scott?"

"My boyfriend. He can't get here till about half seven. He's in his twenties, blond hair and very good-looking. If you see anyone like that, go ahead and introduce yourself."

"I may very well do just that," said Archie. "In the meantime I'll hang around here and hope no one kicks me out."

"See you later," I said, and headed towards the door leading backstage to the dressing rooms. We had been talking in whispers, and I had been as excited as a kid on Christmas Eve. Before going through the door, I turned and gave Archie a wave. He waved back and indicated that he was going over to have a chat with Martin Helgin, who was now on his own. I saw him signal to Martin who was vaguely looking in his direction, and I felt a ridiculous sense of pride that I'd just encouraged two old friends to meet up again. Hopefully after the show I could get Archie and Jimmy together as well.

ARCHIE

"*Now is the winter of our discontent...*" *Richard III* has one of those opening speeches everyone knows. It was all I could do not to speak the lines along with young Mr Knightsbridge. Those same words I'd first spoken the best part of a century ago. Right here.

I paid my ten pounds to a lady at a table by the door who scarcely seemed to care whether I paid her or not. She was chatting away to a middle-aged couple in front of me who paid for their tickets and then started nattering to the box office lady about their holiday. I just slid my ten-pound note across the table and wandered in.

A young man was on stage playing a guitar. Finlay, I think Brooke said. Marching tunes played as if they were ballads. Clearly this wasn't going to be a traditional production in sixteenth century costume. The seats weren't numbered, so I sat on the front row. I remember Sheelagh always used to say, "Archie darling, if you must sit on the front row don't be the one on your own in the middle." Mindful that Brooke might think the same, I sat on the end of the row.

The opening scene. Sophisticated people in evening wear at a party. There was Brooke, dressed attractively in a cocktail dress, holding a glass. Finlay had started playing jazz. By the end of the scene Richard was on his own on stage telling the audience about his plans "*to set my brother Clarence and the King in deadly hate, the one against the other.*"

I looked behind me at the other audience members. Not a bad crowd. About fifty in all. Jimmy Knowles was about four rows back, taking notes. I must have a chat with him later. I'd tried to talk to Martin after wishing Brooke good luck. I waved to him from the lobby and he looked blankly at me before the Churchill woman attracted his attention away. Oh well. I'd probably aged a bit since I last saw Martin. I worked out which was Brooke's boyfriend. Blond hair, on his own, and looking like he felt a bit out of place. I nearly went over to him, but in the end I didn't. After all, what would I say? "Young man, I've been speaking to your young lady every morning for the past two weeks"? If Brooke hadn't told him about me, then that might sound inappropriate. No. I would meet him after the show and Sheelagh would introduce us.

BROOKLYN

I spotted Archie as soon as the lights came up on Act One Scene One. Sitting at the stage left side of the audience on the front row and grinning like an ancient, benign imp. Bless him. When I'd seen him before the show he'd been as excited as a kid going to a birthday party.

Scott had sent me a text at 7.15: *Just arrived. Good luck gorgeous. Watch out for the bunch-backed toad. See, I've read York Notes. I can talk Shakespeare innit. Love Sx.*

Trevor was on blisteringly good form, and our Richard/ Lady Anne scene sparked and crackled with all the intensity of that first time through when I'd stepped in for Rachel.

Rachel. I must contact her. At least to let her know how tonight had gone, and I suppose, to thank her again.

Trevor even got an exit round after that scene, which ends with another of Richard's big speeches: *Shine out fair sun, till I have bought a glass, that I may see my shadow as I pass.*

From where I stood in the wings after that scene, I could see the far end of the front row. There was Archie, clapping as enthusiastically as his frail body would allow. Somehow I knew that he was the one who had made the first clap which started the applause.

ARCHIE

I felt younger than I had in years. The theatre had come back to The Hideaway. Brooke was a superb actress. I was as proud of her then as if I were her grandfather. Or father. Or boyfriend.

When the show finished, I wanted to speak to no one. Not yet anyway. The theatre was back. Here. Where I'd come to school. Where I'd brought Sheelagh when we were newly married, and where we'd turned a village school building into a theatre. I'd built props, and one of them was even in this show. I needed some time alone with my thoughts. So many memories still alive. Even Sheelagh was here in a way. In Brooke. That was very special.

If I spoke to anyone I felt I might cry, and a blubbering fool in an evening suit reeking of mothballs would not be to everyone's taste. So I sat in awed silence after the house lights came up and people started to leave. I had that sense you have after listening to a piece of music. The silence that follows still holds the spirit of the music.

When the theatre was nearly empty I walked slowly out through the lobby. The young blond man, whom I assumed was Scott, was talking with Jimmy Knowles.

I went out into the calm, still evening. The audience were walking away, mostly in pairs to their homes in the village, or to their cars parked in Sea Lion Street or in the church car park.

I was all so like it had been. How it should be. In the old days I would often wait right here for Sheelagh after a first night and we would walk the ten yards over to our house together. So many years. So many memories.

I looked across at our house, silhouetted against the sky. I was standing by the rhododendron bush that for some reason I thought of as mine. Goodness knows why. I hadn't planted it. Illuminated by the pathway lights the leaves looked artificial. Another gust of wind. The bush rustled and moved like a creature stirring. I smiled fondly and touched one of the leaves.

Then I knew. Of course. I hadn't planted it, yet it was mine all the same. How lucky was I to have been here tonight.

TREVOR KNIGHTSBRIDGE

No good at socialising. It's all bollocks anyway. Half the time it's just about arse-licking and getting yourself noticed. OK fine, it has to be done sometimes, but not more than I can help. I prefer talking to people I genuinely like and who genuinely like me, and bollocks to the rest of them.

At school one of my reports had said *Trevor is a quiet boy and should try to contribute more in class.* Thank you Mr Price. Just because I don't gab a lot, doesn't mean I don't think. Dickhead got a shock when I got into uni to read English Lit and then a postgrad course at RADA.

On my own I can be me. Going for a run. In the gym, pumping iron. Reading. I choose my friends carefully. In this cast it's only Trevor George who might become a mate. He's a straightforward nice bloke. Likes cars, same as I do, drives a Toyota. Fair enough, he's got a family, but give me my Jag X-Type any day.

Finlay's alright as well. Great taste in music. Lent me a CD a few days ago. John Murray, yeah he's OK too. Loads I can learn from him just by watching him. Eleanor Boscombe… great actress but she's a bit too prickly for me to get on well with. And then there's Brooklyn. Better actress than Rachel, definitely. Trouble is she's caught me looking at her too often and she clearly doesn't like me. Probably thinks I fancy her.

Being quiet probably makes me seem distant. Sometimes I try and be sociable and then I say the wrong thing and people think I'm weird. I know that. The thing is, I'm better at being other people than I am at being me. Good job I'm an actor then. The trouble is that I'm rubbish at parties. Especially now. After Lynn.

The restaurant had been noisy that night last year. It was a Friday, and there was a stag party. Three tables joined together, and about fifteen blokes behaving like dickheads. So loud you had to shout to make yourself heard. I'd rather have gone to the gym, pumped some iron, and then had a takeaway in front of the TV and *Sportsworld*. Not to be. One of those company meals where everyone wants to be matey. Don't get me wrong. Some of the best friends I've had I've met through theatre work. But you can't force that. If it happens, great. If it doesn't, fuck it. And in a noisy restaurant full of half-pissed blokes and actors trying to impress each other, that's not going to happen.

I like proper conversation about stuff that matters. Shakespeare. Sport. OK, so I'm a bit odd. People tell me I look angry when all I'm doing is thinking about stuff. I just like being on my own. But I was lonely. Alright I know; wanting to be alone and then saying you're lonely: no shit Sherlock, what do you expect?

Except it doesn't work like that. Liking your own company and being comfortable with it doesn't mean you want it to be forced on you. It just means that you avoid parties and events where there's too much chatter and not enough conversation. Like at that company meal for *Deathtrap*. That was one of two thrillers in that season with five other plays. Like I say, it was the *Deathtrap* meal, but the cast of *Rebecca* were there as well. I had been considered for Maxim in *Rebecca*, but I ended up playing Sidney Bruhl in *Deathtrap*.

Something else I like: women. I don't mean just anything in a skirt. But fit, smart, attractive girls. I'd spotted the cute waitress as soon as we'd walked in. Brunette, elfin face, brown eyes, great figure. There were twelve of us at the meal, too many for proper conversation, and I was at the end of the table. So there I was, out of it. Being 'socially inept'. That was how some prat at uni had described me. It was in one of those truth or dare games which I hate, and someone had asked the prat what he thought of Trevor. And the prat had told the truth. Socially inept. Well, fuck him. Last heard, the prat was running a supermarket. Good for him, but why do you need a degree in English Lit to do that?

The cute waitress caught my eye and smiled. A real smile, not a fake are-you-ready-to-order smile. I even ordered a dessert I didn't want, just so I could talk to her. And call her by her name; the name on her badge advertising the restaurant.

"I'll have the coconut and passion fruit ice cream, please Lynn."

A few nights later I was back after rehearsal with Robin East who was in the play with me. He had a swift half and then went back to London for the weekend, leaving me with my pint and my thoughts and doing what I do when I'm on my own in a public place: I watch people. You can tell a lot by just watching. What people are thinking, who they fancy, whether they're happy, depressed, aggressive, whatever. Useful for an actor. Acting Technique at RADA day one: observation of a complete stranger and then portray that person in class. The habit stayed with me. Then suddenly Lynn was there. Crap observation Trevor: I'd been watching a middle-aged guy in a tweed jacket who was a good character study for Lord Peter Wimsey or someone, and I hadn't noticed Lynn coming towards me until she was only six feet away. She sat down. She'd finished work, and would I like to buy her a drink?

Two months later she moved in with me. She brought me out of my shell a bit. Robin said she was one of the few people to actually get me to talk. I like to think that I helped Lynn with some of her problems as well. She'd had a thoroughly crap time and I think I was good for her. Not good enough. Now she was dead.

People talk such a lot of shit when someone close to you dies. "Time is a great healer… It'll get better in time." Maybe; but time is not an anaesthetic. The pain is always there, and it hurts like fuck.

Every hour of every day I think about what happened to her.

That's another thing. People seem to think that just because we'd split up by the time she died, that somehow the pain was going to be less. Ignorant fuckwits. If anything it's worse. Always in my head, fizzing away like white noise, is the thought that if I'd helped her more; been there for her more, then she'd still be here now. I know. Irrational. Probably nothing I could have done except to be more observant. After all, I'm supposed to be good at people-watching. Pity I didn't watch more closely. Pity I hadn't paid closer attention to Rachel Powell.

BROOKLYN

Scott and I walked slowly back to Beth's after the show. The now-familiar walk back along Sea Lion Street which I had walked every morning with Old Bill. Now we were walking deliberately slowly, like teenagers on a date, knowing that when we reached the front door, there would be the long lingering kiss goodnight and then the bashful farewell (*till it be morrow*) that could stretch out for many minutes. Except of course, that we were in our twenties, and we both knew what was going to happen when we got to Beth's house and went to my room with its big double bed and fluffy quilt. The anticipation helped us to enjoy the slow walk home.

In the bar after the show once most of the audience had gone, Jimmy had made a speech thanking everyone and making sure the Cranton Overleigh Institute, Beth Churchill and Martin Helgin were all well and truly thanked in public.

Archie hadn't stayed. I'd been a bit disappointed, but hey, give the old guy a break: at least he came, and at ninety-eight years old he was probably in need of some rest. Back when I'd done *The Seagull* in London, so many of my friends had said they'd come. Most didn't. But this old guy whom I'd only known for two weeks had made an effort, and had been there. And what an effort. Even dressing up specially. To see me. Yes, me. The way he'd looked at me I knew that I was the reason he'd been there. I would go and have a cup of tea with him on Monday before the *Crimewatch* shoot. But tonight was for Scott.

The night was clear and cool. The stars were bright and twinkling in the cloudless sky as we walked hand in hand. "Go on then," I said eventually. "What did you think?"

"Yeah... great. Didn't understand all of it to be honest. Loved the music."

"Yes, Finlay's great," I said. Suddenly I felt very insecure. This was the first play Scott had seen me in and I really needed to hear him say that he liked it. No, not that he liked *it*. That he liked *me*. Feeling about six years old, I blurted out: "So what did you think of me?"

Scott looked surprised, and instantly I wished I hadn't asked.

"Brooklyn, you were great." I must have looked doubtful. Scott went on: "No, really. I couldn't take my eyes off you in that dress."

Oh well. I guess Scott was never going to be my most incisive critic for acting, but at least he fancied me in a cocktail dress. Serves me right for compliment-fishing.

"One thing I don't get though," Scott said; "why did you marry Richard? In that scene over the dead body he was such a creep I felt like punching his lights out."

I tried to explain that that was kind of the point of the scene.

"And that ghost scene near the end was good," said Scott. "You know, the ghostly cocktail party scene that's a bit like the first scene except that the lights all go blue and you all tell Richard to despair and die. Like his past catching up with him, and he couldn't let it go, and you were all saying 'Listen loser, you're not getting away with this, you're going to die.' Really chilling."

Straightaway I felt better. Scott had liked the show, and I was acting like a spoiled kid just because he hadn't been all over me with compliments. Note to self: grow up! My man had driven down from London, probably faster than he should have done, to get here in time for my first night. This was still only his second Shakespeare, and in all fairness, I'm not sure how the Edwardian Palace Theatre Company in Cranton Overleigh would compare with the National Theatre.

We were outside Beth's. "So…" I said, feigning a coy innocence, "would you like to come in for coffee?"

Then we both burst into giggles.

TREVOR KNIGHTSBRIDGE

I always seem to be killing people.

Or having them killed.

I can smile… and murder while I smile.

I can live with that.

Baddies are fun to play. Like now. Playing Richard. Always wanted to play that part.

In *Deathtrap*, my character, Sidney Bruhl, is a writer, who as part of the plot arranges the death of his wife. I won't spoil it for you, but there's a bit more to it than that.

Lynn moved in with me last August, and things were good between us. I don't say much. Neither did she, but it didn't take long for us to start talking about the stuff that mattered. The stuff about her brother. Tom.

Tom was older than Lynn, and the type of kid that parents hope they're not going to have. Headstrong, angry, and if I'm honest, he sounded like an arsehole. But to Lynn, he'd been her big brother whom she hero-worshipped. He'd been done for drug possession; shoplifting, and then had got in with the wrong crowd.

The wrong crowd being one that had included Rachel Powell.

All that had been eight years ago when Rachel was twenty-two. Lynn would have been a schoolgirl.

When Lynn and I met, I was in *Deathtrap* in which Rachel had played my wife. Rachel was OK to work with. Quiet, shy even. That suited me. She was OK as a colleague but that was it. We didn't socialise at all, just did the job. She always knew her lines. No trouble.

Lynn met her a few times socially. After-show parties. Meals, that kind of thing. That was all OK. Until Rachel's name kept coming up in conversation. Unnaturally so. Like Lynn would steer a conversation to include Rachel. Just like a kid in love. And stupid fuckwit that I am, that's what I began to think. What a prat.

Lynn started hanging out with Rachel. At first I thought nothing of it. Just one of my work colleagues who my girlfriend liked better than the others. I was even quite pleased at first. Lynn had had a tough past. Brother in prison. Parents still around, but not close. Lynn was quiet and a bit of a loner. Like me.

Maybe we'd been too alike. Too self-contained.

Lynn and Rachel would meet for a coffee. Shopping trips. Girly nights in round the telly which would usually end with me getting text from Lynn saying she was staying the night. Well, what was I supposed to think? They weren't schoolgirls having a sleepover.

We had row after row about it, which would usually end with me yelling; Lynn in tears and promising that she wouldn't see so much of Rachel. But she always did.

When Lynn moved out, I thought the next thing would be that she would move in with Rachel, and the pair of them would announce they were lesbians. How stupid was I? But then, we all speak perfect hindsight.

Lynn moved back into the flat she'd been in before we got together. She'd told me repeatedly that one day she would tell me about Rachel. But not yet.

By then I was on tour playing Tony in *Dial M for Murder*. That job only finished just before this one. Well, a month or so. You know that story. Hitchcock filmed it: Tony Wendice, an ex-tennis star, plots to murder his wife. I played Tony. See what I mean? I'm always killing people.

BROOKLYN

Scott and I had a traditional Sunday. No, we didn't go to church; I mean we stayed in bed late. Then we had breakfast in Beth's kitchen. Beth was full of praise for the show the night before. The Cranton Overleigh Institute committee were, as she put it, cock-a-hoop about the whole venture and hoped that *Richard III* would be the start of a long-term relationship with Jimmy Knowles and his Palace Theatre. And did I know that there had once been a theatre in that very building, called The Hideaway? And that it had closed years ago, and that since then the village hadn't seemed so lively and how do you learn all those lines, and which do you like best, television or theatre?

Beth was lovely, and wonderfully tolerant, and discreet, about my having Scott here, but now that he was here, and especially as this morning we were both a bit bleary-eyed, I wasn't really up for hearing about the local history, most of which I knew already from Archie. Eventually Beth went away into the conservatory where she was fiddling around with a floral display for the church. But not before she'd signed off with: "Well, I'll leave you two dear people to yourselves, and Scott, you want to hang onto this young lady. She'll be on the telly in no time, and then she'll be off to Hollywood."

She finally left us in peace and we grinned slyly at each other. Me largely because of the Hollywood comment, which in the real world is actually pretty unlikely. Then I noticed Scott was actually blushing. He gave an 'I don't believe it' shake of his head and poured some coffee.

Neither of us said anything, we just held each other's hands, drank our coffee and smiled. We were young. So was our relationship. We were also in love, and serious about each other. Neither of us wanted to spoil what we'd got by 'hanging on' to the other.

We hadn't actually discussed it, but somehow we each knew that that was our unspoken agreement. The day would come when we would have to: if I suddenly found myself with a Hollywood career or if Scott was unexpectedly offered a job in Shanghai or somewhere. For the present, without saying anything, we knew that each of us felt much as we had when we'd had Scott's mate Pete and his wife Gail round to dinner, and Pete, having had too much wine, joked, "So come on then mate, when's the wedding? I need to get planning your stag night." We laughed, and to be fair we'd all had too much to drink, but while we were clearing up after they'd left, Pete's joke still hung in the air like the scent of rain on summer pavements.

Beth's comment was like that, and gave us a thoughtful, fragile silence.

There in his basket, sat Old Bill (Fido). Staring at us with his doggy eyes.

Reading our thoughts.

***

Sunday night. Scott had driven back to London. We'd been out – another trip to Bournemouth for a walk along the beach, then on the way back to Cranton Oh, we pulled up briefly outside the Pelican Club in Port St Catherine so that I could point out the location for the *Crimewatch* shoot.

"After all," I said, "I'll be on the telly before you know it."

Scott chuckled. "I take it you haven't told Beth about that shoot."

I hadn't. Probably just as well, with her 'don't walk through the woods' talk when I'd first arrived.

Now I was up in my room with my laptop and, of course, a glass of red wine and the *Crimewatch* script. There wasn't much to it. A hurriedly drawn storyboard and a list of shots. No lines to learn. Just turn up at the Pelican Club at six, ready for costume and make up. Shoot a scene with me serving customers at a table, then outside into the street for a few shots of me walking down the street. Then a short drive to a layby off the Port St. Catherine road, from where we would walk a few yards to the footpath where the attack had taken place. A few shots there, and the whole thing would be wrapped within a couple of hours.

So tomorrow I had time to kill. Bad choice of words. Tomorrow I had a day off. OK. What to do?

Right. Breakfast. Emails. Maybe touch base with Crispin. Then I'd go down to the Institute and seek out Archie. Actually, no. Change of plan. I'd do that sooner instead of later. Old people could be very set in their ways, and I knew Archie well enough by now to know that his morning routine seemed to revolve around taking Fido for a walk, or Fido taking Archie for a walk. Tomorrow I would accompany him and we would walk Fido together.

I went onto Facebook. *Rachel Powell likes your status* read the text on the drop-down screen. Earlier today, while Scott had been in the shower, I'd updated my status: *Richard III opened last night. Great crowd. My man in the audience. Here's to a great tour. One down, twenty-two to go.*

I started to type a reply to Rachel and then thought better of it. I wouldn't say I'm particularly cautious, but sometimes there are things that are better expressed as private messages rather than written on the Facebook wall where anyone can see them. So I clicked on the private message icon so I could send Rachel a message that wouldn't be seen by prying eyes. That wouldn't be seen by people like Trevor Knightsbridge, who always seemed to be watching people.

Hi Rachel, been meaning to contact you. How's it all going? First night was great, Jimmy's alright really, and tomorrow I've got a small TV job on Crimewatch. Nothing much, but a start I guess.

A reply came back immediately: *Hi Brooke, that's great. Hoping to see the show sometime, but I'll keep a low profile coz I don't want JK or even Derek to see me. I'll be in Port St C tomorrow. Fancy meeting for lunch?*

Now that was a question. Well, what else would I do with most of the day?

Sure, that'd be great, I wrote.

***

I awoke as usual to Radio 4, and was down in Beth's kitchen having breakfast soon after nine, feeling good that I was up and about, and also that I had a day off. Love my job, but love days off as well. This morning I'd go and see Archie. I was looking forward to seeing him and hearing his verdict on the show and whether he thought it had what Martin Helgin had called 'the Stephens factor', then I would meet Rachel for lunch at the Crown and Anchor near the Eddy Pally, and then tonight would be the *Crimewatch* shoot.

It was a beautifully clear spring day with just a hint of a chill in the air as Fido and I took our usual walk along Sea Lion Street to the hall. Only this time there was no hurry, and no need to buy sandwiches at Bateman's. We'd left the set and lights up on Saturday night and the plan was that tomorrow morning, Tuesday, we would all meet here at eleven, load everything into the van, and then set out for our next venue on the tour, near Dorchester. But today there was no rush.

Archie, for once, wasn't waiting outside his house for us. But then he wasn't expecting me today. I stopped by the porch. The door was ajar, as always, the kitchen with no lights on, but just lit by daylight through the cobwebbed, dusty windows.

"Hello," I called out softly. This was feeling like a re-run of that day when we'd been unloading the van, and I'd paid Archie a visit. He'd heard my voice and had thought I was Sheelagh, and then he'd come out and told me he was 'agreeably well'. Bless him.

"Archie, it's Brooke," I called again.

No answer. I looked back at Fido who was just waiting by the door out in the sunshine, panting gently and looking at me with patient eyes.

I looked around, and noticed for the first time how grimy everything was. An old sink and kitchen units that might have been the latest thing in the 1960s. No cooker in sight. Not even a fridge.

Again, like before, I felt like an intruder, and I really didn't want to frighten Archie if he was asleep or had just dozed off in the lounge. Of course he may have just gone for a walk, or he might even be over in the hall, taking the set down. That would be just like him, especially after his antics earlier in rehearsals when he'd set up the lights single-handedly. Of course, that was it.

I went out into the sunshine and over to the hall. Locked. I peered through the door into the lobby. No sign of anyone.

I was beginning to feel worried. A ninety-eight-year-old living alone, and one who clearly led a fairly quiet, reclusive life. Thinking about it, there was a good chance that he'd just passed away in the night. Occasionally you hear stories about an old person, living alone, who dies and then isn't found for days or even weeks. I had a chilling thought that I was about to be the one to find Archie dead in his bed.

I walked back across the path to the house. Fido was just sitting by the door. If he'd been sitting next to a gramophone it would have looked like an old poster for His Master's Voice.

"Archie!" I called again, louder. "It's Brooke. I've come to see you."

Silence.

I walked back into the small hallway and gently pushed a dark green door that I guessed led into the lounge. Through the window, past some very grubby net curtains, I could see the hall and the path leading out to the road. A table, covered in dust, with a pair of wooden chairs either side, also covered in dust. A faded leather armchair that had the look of being a 'favourite' chair. The place didn't look like anyone actually lived here, even though the armchair's seat still had the imprint of someone having sat there.

Back into the hall, and to the stairs. I climbed them as gently as if each step was mined. Narrow, straight up to the landing. "Archie! Are you there? It's Brooke." I could hear the panic rising in my voice. Two doors were in front of me. Gently, I turned the handle on the first one and opened it towards me.

And screamed.

A broom toppled out and hit me. This wasn't a room, but a cupboard of some sort.

The next door. The bedroom. Where I was convinced I would find Archie dead in his bed. My heart was thumping through my chest as I pushed the door slowly open. The curtains were open. Actually, there were no curtains. Or any furniture, or even a carpet. Just an empty room. With a door on the other side, presumably leading to the next bedroom.

Feeling mystified, and also foolish, I checked that room as well.

Empty. Just like the other room. The whole house had the feeling of having been abandoned long ago.

I breathed deeply to calm myself down, and let out a long sigh. Almost like doing a voice exercise. OK. So no one was here. *Right. Calm down.*

I went outside into the sunshine feeling like the victim of some strange practical joke. I looked down at Fido who was still sitting patiently by the door. He cocked his head to one side and made one of those plaintive doggy squeaks.

"Archie's not here, Fido," I said, bending down and giving him a pat, hearing a slight tremor in my voice. "Do you know where he is?" The dog gave a slight quiver and reached out with one paw as if he was shaking hands. Then, as if making up his mind, he went off for his walk on his own, just as I'd seen him do with Archie. Down through the garden, and into the woods.

And that was the last time Old Bill went for a walk through the woods.

***

I stood there for several minutes wondering what on earth to do next. I got out my phone and considered calling the police. Or maybe check around the nearby hospitals. I would have done it too, but the state of Archie's house had really thrown me. This was not a house that had the look of being lived in. Not for years. It had a deserted, dead feel to it.

Yet I had seen Archie in the house, and outside when he had clearly only just come out through the front door.

I wandered vaguely over to the hall door and looked through again in the vain hope of seeing Archie inside.

No one.

Slowly I retraced my steps back to the road. When I reached the gateway I noticed Martin Helgin from the Institute's committee coming towards me. He recognised me straightaway. "Morning Brooklyn," he said, and then with surprise, "You're not working today are you?"

"No… I, er…"

"Quite right. I should think you need a couple of days off after Saturday. Great show. I'm sure Beth's told you how pleased everyone is," said Martin.

"Yes she has. I was wondering—"

"Good, yes, well you were very good. That actor who played Richard was excellent wasn't he? Don't know how you manage to remember all those lines."

"Thank you, that's kind," I said, and then, feeling I had to take charge of the conversation, "Martin, I was wondering if you knew where Archie was?"

"Who?" said Martin, looking puzzled.

"You know, you were talking to him before the show on Saturday."

Martin still looked puzzled "No, I don't think so… I did speak to a lot of people mind you. It's the way of these things. When you've been on the committee as long as I have everyone seems to think you know everything. As the saying goes: 'The buck stops here.'" He smiled a gentle, seventy-year-old man smile. "Tell you what, why don't you join me in a cup of tea? I was just going to check on the Institute, mainly because I left my reading glasses in the kitchen. Had a senior moment when I was locking up."

By this time we were walking slowly back towards the hall, past Archie's house.

"Yes, you remember," I said, "we were talking about the show, and you said you hoped the play had the Stephens factor."

"Ah yes," said Martin, "I remember saying that, and then you went off to talk to someone else."

I said, "Yes, that's right; well the someone else was Archie. I chatted to him for a couple of minutes, then I said I needed to get backstage and he told me that he was going to have a word with you."

Martin was looking at me blankly.

"He even waved at you just as he was walking over to you," I added lamely.

"No, young lady, I don't remember that at all. I think the next person I spoke to was Beth Churchill. As I say though, it was a busy night."

I was going to get no sense at all out of Martin. "Right, OK, not to worry," I said, and then with a confidence I didn't feel, "I'm sure he'll turn up."

I hadn't the first idea what to do next. Maybe I'd been mistaken. Perhaps Archie lived elsewhere in the village and just liked to visit the place where he used to live, and somewhere in his mind, he still did live in the house that had once been his. This suddenly seemed to be a likely explanation. Maybe that day, when we'd been unloading the van and I'd gone in and spoken to him, he had just happened to be there, reminiscing.

I wandered vaguely back in the direction of Beth's house turning all this over in my mind, and scanning the nearby houses trying to decide in which one of them Archie might have rented a room, or even if one of them was some kind of sheltered housing or old folks' home. Then, abruptly, I took out my phone and dialled Crispin's number. I needed something normal to focus my mind, and there was nothing like work to do that. After all, I did have a job to do this evening.

"Hi Crispin, it's Brooke."

"Darling! Sweetie! Lovely! How did it go the other night? I raised a glass to you at half past seven."

"It was great," I said truthfully, "quite a good audience. Scott came down, which was great. Right now I'm out for a walk and making the most of my day off before tonight. Just thought I'd touch base with you."

"Well lovely, it's always a treat to hear your dulcet tones, but I'm up to my eyelashes in submissions. The usual backlog from the weekend. There's a couple of things you would have been right for but I can't sub you because you're not really available till after your tour. Oh well, *c'est la vie, ma cherie!*"

We chatted for a bit, although I could tell that Crispin was indeed very busy and anxious to crack on with submitting his other clients for jobs on his Spotlight link. He wished me well for the shoot tonight and told me that he'd be sure to watch the programme when it aired the following week. On Thursday. In all the excitement of getting *Richard III* up and running, and with the stress of making sure I could do the *Crimewatch* shoot without any conflict with Jimmy, I'd forgotten to ask when the programme would be on TV. Thursday. We would be in Guildford. Oh well. I could get someone to record it for me I guess.

My chat with Crispin had the desired effect. I was still puzzled about what had become of Archie, but for the moment, that would have to wait. Having spoken to Crispin I was suddenly in the mood to chat to old friends; and if

I'm honest, phoning my agent when I was actually working made me feel like a 'proper' actress. Next on the list was Duncan Ward. He'd emailed me to say he couldn't come to the opening night, but would try to catch the show on tour somewhere. I doubted that he would. He would want to of course, but promises to see a show being done by a friend in the business are very easy to make, but quite hard to keep. Life is busy, diaries get full, especially when you're freelance, and you have to schedule various types of work in order to earn a crust.

Duncan answered on the third ring. "Hi Brooke, I thought about you on Saturday, how was it?"

"It was fab thanks. Thanks again for giving me the nod about this job," I said, gushingly.

"No problem, but don't forget it was you that got the job. And you that impressed Jimmy enough to give you Lady Anne. So I will let you buy me a half, but not a whole pint." He laughed.

We chatted for a while about the job and then, as he hadn't been there on Saturday night, just before ending the call I said, "Anyway, it was a shame you weren't there because I'd been hoping to reacquaint you with Archie Stephens."

There was a slight pause, then: "What, you mean they've put the picture of him up or something?"

My brain felt like a computer with a slow internet connection. "No... I, er..."

But not hearing my uncertainty, Duncan went on: "There was talk of it. A local artist did a portrait of him just before he died, but for some reason it was never put up. Instead they planted a big bush right by the door of the old theatre and put a plaque there."

I was too stunned to speak.

"Brooke?" said Duncan. "Are you still there?"

"Yes, sorry Duncan," I said. Even though the sun was up and it was one of those spring days that feel more like summer, I felt cold.

"Are you sure?" he said.

"Yes… it's just, I met an old guy called Archie, and I thought—"

Duncan laughed kindly. "No my love. Archie Stephens died about ten years ago, so whoever your old guy was, it certainly wasn't him. They did a kind of memorial service for him outside the old theatre and planted a bush or something. I wasn't there, but I kept in touch with Eleanor for a bit and she told me. Years ago now. You would have been choosing your GCSEs."

Desperately trying to hold my emotions in, I passed off my 'mistake' as a simple confusion, said a breezy goodbye to Duncan and ended the call.

I stared blindly at my phone. Then at the street. What was happening to me? I went uncertainly back towards the hall. Maybe Martin Helgin was still there. But I wasn't sure I wanted to speak to anyone just yet.

This just didn't feel right. Archie had been there. I had spoken to him on several occasions. He had taken Fido for a walk. I had even smelled the mothball scent on his suit. He had set up the stage lights and some scenery and had been as pleased with his efforts as a toddler wanting to show his parents a model he'd made. I just didn't believe I'd seen a ghost.

I walked up the pathway to what had been The Hideaway Theatre. The rhododendron bush was bright in the sunlight. My eyes searched the wall next to the door.

There.

A dull and faded bronze plate screwed into the brickwork with the inscription:

IN AFFECTIONATE AND LOVING MEMORY OF
ARCHIE STEPHENS
1916–2004
WHO WITH HIS WIFE SHEELAGH RAN
THE HIDEAWAY THEATRE IN THIS BUILDING.

OLD BILL

The Young One was in the Warm Drink Man's house for a long time. Fido could have told her he wasn't there. As soon as he walked up the path he knew the Ancient Scent had gone. He just sat by the door to wait for her to find out.

He had gone. Sad. People do that. They just go. Fido held out his leg for the Young One to hold. He wanted her to be happier.

One day the Young One would go too. He liked the Young One. She calls him Fido. She's the only one who ever made share-thinking noises with the Warm Drink Man for many long-a-year. Maybe that's why the Warm Drink Man went. Perhaps he liked doing share-thinking noises and wanted to go where more people would. The Floppy Clothes Lady never did. Perhaps nobody except the Young One liked the Warm Drink Man enough to make share-thinking noises.

Fido went for the walk they always took, but somehow knew today he would not come back. Today he had to take the usual walk.

To where the Bad Thing had happened.

BROOKLYN

Back at Beth's, I went to my room and the tears came almost before I had time to muffle the sound in the duvet. I felt bereaved, hurt, disappointed, and strangely frightened all at the same time. Did I believe in ghosts? I don't know; it was something I'd never even thought about. Not seriously. I was now faced with the possibility that I really had formed a friendship with somebody who quite literally hadn't existed for over ten years.

Suddenly I knew the person I needed more than anyone. Scott. I phoned him.

He answered straightaway. "Hi Brooklyn. So you didn't fancy another lie-in then?"

I laughed as lightly as I could manage, but he picked up the strangeness in my voice right away.

"You OK?" he asked.

"Well, kind of… I don't know. Look, you know when you came to see the show?"

"Yes?" he said, and I could hear the puzzlement in his voice.

"Well, sitting right at the front on the end of the row was an old guy."

"Oh yes," said Scott, "Jimmy. We had a chat afterwards."

"No, I don't mean Jimmy. This guy was much older. In his late nineties."

"No," said Scott, "didn't see anyone like that. Not on the front row anyway."

"Yes, he was right on the end of the row, grinning like the Cheshire Cat all the way through," I said.

"No, definitely not. In fact I remember the front two rows were completely empty. I didn't want to sit there because I didn't want to put you off. The only person in front of me a few seats away was Jimmy." There was a long pause. "Brooklyn, what is it? You sound upset."

So I told him.

***

Scott and I talked for about half an hour, and to give credit where it's due, he didn't tell me I was being silly or anything like that.

When I'm upset I can be a bit like my mum and tell you the same information several times in different ways. Dad, bless him, then tries to comfort Mum, but she's not ready to be comforted and they end up arguing because she tells him he doesn't understand.

Scott just listened. At first I could hear office sounds in the background. Phones ringing, the background chatter of the office. Then this was replaced by traffic noise. He'd walked outside into Fenchurch Street, where the background noise was louder, but he wouldn't be overheard by his colleagues who would then ask awkward questions.

Eventually he said, "Brooklyn darling, I've got to get back, but try not to make yourself upset."

I said, "How can I not be upset? I'm fairly sure I've seen a ghost."

"I know love, you said that."

"No, listen" – *oh God, I sound like my mum* – "he was as real as anyone else standing there. I mean, I could even smell—"

"The mothballs he'd hung up his suit in, I know," said Scott. "Listen, love. I've really got to get back to work. We'll talk later, yeah? Call me after the TV shoot tonight."

We'd ended the call, although not with our usual sign-off. I still had a couple of hours before I needed to set off to meet Rachel, so I did a Google search for Archie Stephens, and after a few false starts I found some of the history of The Hideaway Theatre and Archie and Sheelagh Stephens. Mostly they were articles written by local historians which had appeared in limited print runs of local history books.

What Duncan had told me was pretty accurate. Sheelagh had died quite suddenly in 1991 when she was sixty-five. She'd been sitting in the lounge reading a script, had dozed off and slipped quietly away. Archie had been over in the theatre fiddling with some props, then had come over to the house, asked her if she'd like a cup of tea, and then hadn't been able to wake her up.

Archie's obituary from *The Stage*, April 10th 2004, read:

It is with much sadness that we learnt of the death of Archie Stephens, who died peacefully in hospital after a short illness at the age of eighty-eight. Mr Stephens was born in 1916 and grew up in the village of Cranton Overleigh in Dorset where as a boy, he attended the village school. The school building was eventually bought by Mr and Mrs Stephens, and after some modest conversion work, was opened as a repertory theatre in 1949.

Archie Stephens served as a second lieutenant in the Navy in the war years, and was demobbed in 1946 at the age of thirty. After a brief career as a journalist for the Daily Express, he brought his wife Sheelagh for a weekend away to the town where he had grown up, and almost on a whim, the couple bought the old school hall. Ladies and gentlemen of a certain age will remember Sheelagh's various performances at the theatre, and many in our profession hold fond memories of Archie and Sheelagh running their little theatre just off the beaten track in a village only six miles from the south coast. Following Sheelagh's tragic early death in 1991, Archie found it increasingly hard to cope with her loss, and The Hideaway Theatre only played one more season. The theatre building was then sold to the trustees of the Cranton Overleigh Institute and has functioned as a successful village hall ever since. Mr Stephens continued to live in the house beside the hall, and would often be seen talking to visitors, regaling them with tales of the theatre's history and, in the case of the 3rd Dunslinton Sea Scouts troop, giving them advice on sailing, and telling them stories of his years in the Navy.

Archie was never an actor, far preferring the management of the theatre. Never one to shy away from difficult decisions, he had a reputation for harsh criticism, and intolerance of incompetence or sloppy behaviour. It was my great good fortune to get to know Archie in his declining years and I always enjoyed his many visits to the Palace Theatre, where he was generous with his time, and clear-sighted in his advice.

Many in our profession had their first job at The Hideaway Theatre, and those who knew him well, will remember him as a wise and gentle man.

James Knowles

The line about *a reputation for harsh criticism, and intolerance of incompetence or sloppy behaviour* could have been a description of Jimmy just as much as of Archie. Not only had Jimmy Knowles written Archie's obituary, he had also made a speech at Archie's memorial service after which there had been the planting of the rhododendron bush and the unveiling of the plaque outside the hall. Somewhere in the Edwardian Palace

Theatre, a seat had been dedicated to Archie. I reckon it would be somewhere near the front.

***

It wasn't till I was on the bus to the Seafront to meet Rachel at the Crown and Anchor, that I realised Old Bill hadn't come back to Beth's from his morning walk. The last I'd seen of him was when he'd plodded his way through Archie's garden into the woods. I told myself he was probably OK. After all, I didn't know how long his walks with Archie had taken. Half an hour? All morning?

I remember when I was a kid my parents had sent me off on a camping holiday with the Guides. I was only about eleven, but I've never forgotten the advice our leader had given us about what to do if we ever felt unhappy or homesick: find a friend. Well, I wasn't exactly homesick, but this morning had left me feeling emotionally ragged. So by the time I got to the Crown and Anchor I was really looking forward to seeing Rachel.

We sat at a table by the window and ordered lunch. It was one of those 'two for £6.99' deals some pubs do, so we had fish and chips and shared a bowl of onion rings.

Over a drink while we were waiting for our food I asked, "How was the screen test or whatever?"

"I don't really know yet, but I'm still in the running," said Rachel. "I had a day at Pinewood last week shooting an action scene as a test. Sorry, I can't tell you much or it would give it away and I'm sworn to secrecy, but let's just say there will be a lot of green screen and special effects."

"Cool."

"Yeah, it kind of is, but actually you'd be surprised how

ordinary it all seems once you're there. Just people doing a job. Anyway, how are you doing in my role?"

"Loving it. Absolutely loving it."

"And Jimmy?"

"He's OK. He actually told me how much he liked my work."

"Really?" Rachel looked surprised.

"Yes, he… well, he said I was doing really well as Lady Anne," I said weakly, remembering, but not wanting to mention, "You're more than twice the actress she is."

"Wow, that is rare. Praise from Caesar," said Rachel. "He must really like you. How about Trevor?"

"He's OK I guess. A bit weird," I said. Rachel was watching me knowingly. "OK, actually he gives me the creeps," I admitted.

Rachel grinned broadly. Our food arrived and we swapped Trevor Knightsbridge stories. Like the other week, it felt as though we were schoolgirls sharing confidences.

"I thought for a while I was the only one who had a problem with him," said Rachel. "I mean, give the guy his due, he's a bloody good actor, but he's a bit… well… scary. You never really know where you are with him. I mean, like when we were doing *Deathtrap* he was always reliable onstage, but offstage, just a bit…"

"A bit of a cold fish." I completed Rachel's sentence for her.

"Exactly. I'd watch your back with him if I were you. I mean, the way he just stares at you when you're talking to him. Actually it did all get a bit scary. I mean like we are now, you know, just having lunch. Well, I was quite friendly with his girlfriend for a while, and it was sometimes like he was stalking us. You know, like watching our every move. For instance we'd be sitting in a place like this, and then he'd turn up. If he saw us, he'd come over and act all surprised, but sometimes he'd just be there, thinking we hadn't seen him. And then… no, I'm not sure I should tell you."

"It's OK, I think I'm unshockable," I said.

"Well, alright. One night Lynn was at my place up in Guildford, we were having a girly night in, and we noticed Trevor was outside. Just watching the flat. Sitting in his car."

"Lynn? What, you mean—"

"Yes, the girl who died."

Of course it was logical that Rachel would have known Lynn. She and Trevor had worked for Jimmy before, and Lynn had been a local girl. I just hadn't made the connection before now.

"Are you OK?" asked Rachel.

"Yes, just… I didn't think you'd known her. I mean… what was she like?"

"She looked a lot like you actually."

I sighed wearily. "Yeah, I know. Creepy Trev told me. Just what I needed."

Rachel went on. "Character-wise she was a bit… sly."

"Sly?" I asked.

"Yeah, like she was always looking out for something. Or someone. And once she got her teeth locked on she would never let go. You know, like a ferret. I reckon she and Trev were quite a good match actually. Well, she got her ferret teeth into him anyway. Except I think she bit off more than she could chew. I think Trevor could be dangerous, whereas Lynn, well, she clearly wasn't."

"You don't mean…?" I couldn't quite bring myself to speak the unspeakable thought that Trevor might have killed Lynn Arthur.

Rachel knew what I meant. "No," she said slowly. There was a long pause. Too long. "Not really." Rachel was just staring out of the window. "The guy's a creep, but that's probably all."

There was another long silence. Each of us thinking things we were afraid to share. A silence that shimmered with the delicate danger of terrible thoughts finding their voice. Time to change the subject to something lighter, less threatening. I'd had enough heavy stuff for one morning.

"So when did you decide to become an actress?" I asked through a mouthful of cod in breadcrumbs.

"I don't know really. It was a slow process. I did a few of what you might call community theatre projects, and I caught the bug from them. How about you?"

"About as long ago as I can remember," I said, "and finally, a whole year after graduating, it's actually starting to happen, partly thanks to you, and I'm loving it. I'm even working tonight."

"Really? I thought today was a day off."

"It is, but I've got a BBC shoot for *Crimewatch*."

"That's great Brooke, what are you doing in it?"

"Well, as you know, I look a bit like this Lynn Arthur girl, so I got the job on a reconstruction at the place where she worked, and at the place where she died. In the woods."

"Oh… right," said Rachel, rather strangely. Well, I didn't blame her. She had known Lynn after all.

"It's a bit weird really," I said. "It wouldn't be so bad if I wasn't working down here. You know, like if I'd just got the *Crimewatch* job, and had to come down from London for the shoot. As it is, working right near where she died, and getting to know people who knew her, it kind of feels like it was all planned, but not in a good way."

Rachel was still looking at me in a strangely distant way. "A bit like you're a ghost of someone's past that won't go away," she said, once I'd run out of words to try to describe how I felt.

Ghost. That word hit me like a slap before waking. I must have looked shocked.

Rachel asked, "You OK?"

I came within a breath of telling Rachel about Archie, and how I believed I had seen a real ghost, but just then the waiter came over and asked if our meals were alright, and by the time we'd ordered a Diet Pepsi and an orange and soda, the moment had passed.

***

After lunch, Rachel went to her former digs to pick up some stuff before driving back to Guildford where she lived. She ended up inviting me back to her place in a week or so, after we'd played our gig at Guildford's Yvonne Arnaud Theatre. Despite her confidence and obvious success, there was something a bit needy about her, and so I agreed, partly because I thought she might be hurt if I hadn't, and also, to be honest, because she said she'd record my *Crimewatch* appearance so we could watch it over what she called a "cheeky glass of wine" – presumably one with a silly grin and a range of snappy one-liners. I could just as easily catch *Crimewatch* on BBC iPlayer, but it was kind of her to offer, so I said OK.

At only 2.30 in the afternoon I still had a few hours to kill before I had to be at the Pelican Club, so I went to the Edwardian Palace Theatre and had a coffee I didn't really want in the cafe, just for something to do. I needed to think about everything that had happened today. Having lunch with Rachel had helped a bit, but now I was on my own, the strange events of the morning were still there like guests at a party who don't know when to leave. I finished my coffee and went through the 'staff only' door in the cafe that would take me to the foot of the stairs leading up to Gemma's office. There was something I had to ask her.

After knocking timidly on her door (*I hate that my default setting seems to be apologetic timidity*), I went in and asked, "Gemma, I've got a strange request: do you happen to know where in the theatre there is a seat dedicated to Archie Stephens?"

The few times I had met Gemma I'd found her a little prickly, but today she seemed in a reasonable mood: "Ooooh, now you're asking. I think it's in one of the side boxes next to the stage. Why do you ask?"

Stupidly, I wasn't prepared for that question. "I was, you know, just surfing on the internet about this history of this place, and he sounded an interesting guy. Just curious, that's all."

"Pop in and have a look if you must," said Gemma. "Happy hunting."

I went into the theatre. That evening there was no show, but the houselights were on. I eventually found the small brass plaque on one of four seats in the box closest to the stage on the stage-right side:

Archie Stephens
Rest easy Gentle Sir
Enjoy the show

OLD BILL

After the Young One had discovered the Warm Drink Man was no longer there, Old Bill had gone into the woods and followed his usual route along the path where he'd walked with the Warm Drink Man. Where sometimes he saw the Quick Panting Man.

Where he had seen the person with the Cain Scent.

Now he sat, like he often did, and watched the world go by. Except now he sat near where the Bad Thing had happened. Where the people in white clothes and their white tent had been.

Why he did this, why he had to do this, was because of The Ripple.

The Ripple is why cows lie down before it rains. Why birds migrate in winter. Why starlings fly together in flocks that move like clouds. You don't understand The Ripple. You feel it.

Provided you are not a human. They know nothing of The Ripple. Only creatures feel The Ripple.

Without actually knowing what it is.

It was something in The Ripple which had made Old Bill go with the Young One to The Warm Drink Man's house every morning. And it was something in The Ripple which made him plod his slow way to where the Bad Thing had happened.

And wait.

TREVOR KNIGHTSBRIDGE

It wasn't really the way I wanted to spend my Monday night. But then people have different ways of dealing with things. You try to get on with life after someone close to you dies, and it's fucking hard. Our relationship had ended, but even so I haven't been here much in the past few months. Not since Lynn and I broke up.

I'd just started to come to terms with the break-up when Lynn died. This job was helping with that, or so I thought, but then this girl Brooklyn turns up and not only walks around looking like Lynn, but then gets asked by the BB fucking C to pretend to be Lynn for fucking *Crimewatch.* To be fair I don't think I've been much help. She's noticed me looking at her too much.

Like I said. Not really how I wanted to spend my evening. In the Pelican Club trying to stay unnoticed, while the small film crew from the Beeb films their shots for *Crimewatch.* I had a drink just to have something to hold, and waited, sitting at a table on the other side of the club from where the management had roped off a small section. For the next hour or so the crew were coming in, adjusting lights, trying out camera angles and consulting notes and a storyboard.

That policeman who'd asked me the questions was there too. Nice bloke actually, a bit younger than me. Paul somebody. He'd asked me about Lynn: what was she like, did I have any idea why someone might have attacked her? Why had we broken up? I guess he's hanging around the shoot in case the whole thing jogs anyone's memory. Hope it does.

When it was about half past six I ordered some food. I didn't want to be seen. But I did want to see Brooklyn.

No… Lynn. I wanted to see Lynn. Just once more. My last memories of her aren't great. The arguments we had. The tears.

I should add that the tears were mine.

Surprised, right? I thought you would be. I was angry with myself. Angry for losing my temper. I was such a prat. A stupid, testosterone-charged, alpha male prat.

She'd kept saying she'd 'tell me about Rachel', and in my head the reason was that they were having some sort of affair. I know, why did I think that? How could I think that when Lynn had shared my bed? I'll tell you why: because I was a prat. Too stuck on Lynn to see clearly.

I found out eventually of course. But not from Lynn. By then it was all too late and so my last memories were of arguments, shouting. Then pictures in the paper, and worst of all, my imagination of what she might have looked like. Do you really need me to spell it out?

No. Thought not.

I needed a better picture in my head to remember her by. The ones my imagination feeds me rise in my mind like fucking Banquo. The ghosts that exist in real life are called memories. Good ones, bad ones; sometimes scary ones.

Time to replace some of the bad ones with something better. A memory of Lynn as she was. I would lay her ghost to rest.

BROOKLYN

At quarter to six in the evening the taxi arrived at Beth's to take me down into Port St Catherine for the *Crimewatch* shoot. I came back on the bus after my visit to Archie's seat in the theatre, and spent an hour or so trying to switch off from everything that had happened during the day. A couple of *Friends* episodes had helped with that.

It was a drizzly damp evening, and the parade of shops and restaurants which included the Pelican Club looked prettier than usual because the lights were reflecting in the wet pavement.

I thanked my taxi driver and went inside the Pelican Club. A girl of about my age with bright ginger hair, freckles and an easy smile came up to me.

"Hi, Brooklyn, I'm Josie, the first AD."

My mind raced. AD? Yes, of course. Assistant Director.

"Right, we'll get you through costume and make up and then we should be good to go. Can I get you a drink or anything?" said Josie.

"Yes, thanks, a Coke'd be great."

Josie quickly introduced me to the rest of the crew. It was one of those introductions where you try very hard to quickly memorise names and faces while knowing that in two minutes' time you won't have a clue who is who. The cameraman was either Nick or Mick, I'm still not quite sure, and the director was a birdy-looking man in his thirties called Goran, who had an Eastern European accent. Then there was a policeman in a high-vis jacket, who Josie introduced as Constable Paul Blake, who was going to hang around in case anyone remembered something important.

"Don't worry," said Paul with a smile, "I was hoping to be on the telly but I'll keep out of your way."

Josie took me to what I supposed was the club manager's office through a 'staff only' door. "Here we are," she said. "We've got you a top and a skirt to put on, and then for all the outside shots we've got you a trenchcoat very similar to the one the murdered girl was wearing."

I must have looked troubled because she suddenly said, "You OK with all this?"

"Yes, sorry… yes of course. I've just had a bit of a strange day, that's all."

"OK, cool, right. I'll get you your Coke, and then Cheryl will be in to get you made up, and to do something with your hair. We've got a couple of extras to be the people you serve at the table, and she's just doing them first."

OK Brooke, come on, concentrate.

I changed into the dark pencil skirt and light purple blouse that was the uniform for the Pelican Club. Together with the medium high heels and bright red lipstick, the effect was a glamorous, sophisticated, secretarial look which was quite 1950s, and very sexy in an understated way.

Cheryl was in her forties, and wearing bib-type overalls as a fashion statement. She spent a few minutes applying make up, and then somewhat longer rearranging my hair to resemble Lynn's.

"There you are Brooke, I think you'll do," she said. *I think you'll do.* Just what I'd said to Archie the other night when he wanted my approval for his evening suit. That thought came at me like an unexpected arrow. I must have looked startled, as I caught Cheryl looking at me strangely.

"Great, thanks Cheryl," I said, hoping I sounded normal.

"I can see why you got the job," said Cheryl, you look just like the murdered girl. Terrible story, that."

No one had so far referred to Lynn Arthur by name. She was 'the murdered girl'. At least to Cheryl and to Josie.

I looked in the long mirror which had been placed in the room and stared at myself. No, I looked at her. The girl who looked like me. The girl whose memory had been in my life for a fortnight. The girl creepy Trevor saw whenever he looked at me.

Lynn Arthur.

TREVOR KNIGHTSBRIDGE

I'd driven here, so I was on the zero alcohol lager. Some brands taste like piss, but the Cobra Zero on sale in the Pelican Club was quite good. Goes down very easily as well. Especially with a curry. I wasn't expecting to enjoy tonight much, so I thought I'd make it as bearable as possible with the addition of cold beer and curry. Beef madras. Not as good as what you get at the Jewel of the Raj on the Seafront. But OK.

I was just getting started on my curry, and was on my third beer of the evening, when she appeared.

Lynn.

Credit to the make-up lady and the costume. Brooklyn looked just like her. I like women wearing heels as well. Puts everything on display much better. Brooklyn even had Lynn's walk. But then in heels, most birds do.

I didn't want her to see me. Didn't want to freak her out. I needed to get rid of some ghosts in my life, not to scare a work colleague who already didn't like me. So I deliberately sat on the far side of the restaurant. There was a pillar between me and the camera crew, so I would only see what was going on in odd glimpses. There were enough other people in the restaurant for me to remain inconspicuous and one or two had gone up to the crew to ask them what was going on, and would they be on the telly? I kept my eyes down and only looked over occasionally.

Trouble was, I had a job to keep my eyes off her. *For fuck's sake Trev, get a grip.* She was gorgeous. Actually, no. Brooklyn wasn't. She didn't do much for me in that way at all. But Lynn did… had. It's weird. They looked alike, but with Brooklyn there was no chemistry. On stage yeah, we could act that, but in real life forget it. Lynn had been different. Chemistry from the start.

They were lining up the first shot. A couple were sat at a table and Lynn was about to serve their drinks and ask what they wanted to order. I had to smile. Brooklyn had never done waitressing. You could tell by the way she questioned one of the real waitresses who the director called over for advice, and because she had to be taught how to hold the tray. The first time, she could have been a ten-year-old serving tea at a village fete. There was none of the practised ease, and even grace, of the experienced waitress.

I made myself look away and positioned the plastic-coated menu like an open book in front of me so I could stay out of sight.

Stay invisible.

BROOKLYN

If I'm honest with myself I quite liked the attention. The Pelican Club was about two-thirds full. Meals being served. Couples having a quiet glass of wine. There was a white piano in the corner which I guess got used on Friday nights, but tonight was unmanned. Instead we were the star attraction. Josie did a very effective job of politely turning people away when they asked what we were doing and when was it going to be on the telly.

I enjoyed the feeling of importance. People glancing over to look at me. Wondering if I was famous. Wondering where they had seen me before. Where they had seen 'me' before was probably on the front of a newspaper, or on *News at Ten*.

As it turned out, we weren't recording much sound, and Goran said that the likelihood is that they'd use a 'wild track' and that the whole scene would probably just have a voice-over. Just for safety though, Rick, the sound guy, wired me up with a lapel mike and together with the two extras, who I was supposed to be serving, I improvised a little dialogue along the lines of "Are you ready to order?"

I had to hold quite still while Rick was positioning the microphone in such a way that it wouldn't be seen. Eventually it was decided that clipped into my collar would be best, with the wire going down my back. This led to quite a lot of clumsy untucking of my blouse from the skirt in order to feed the wire through.

It was while this was going on that I saw Trevor. Creepy Trevor. On his own, over the other side of the restaurant.

The menu propped up in front of him like a barrier. He was shovelling in a mouthful of rice so he didn't see me looking. I looked away quickly, my mind racing. What was he doing here? He must have known tonight was the *Crimewatch* shoot. He wasn't with anyone, so he clearly wasn't here to socialise. So why? To see me? No, not very likely. He didn't like me much, and to be fair I'd been a bit cool with him over the past few days.

OK. Let's give the guy a break. Maybe he just always comes here. Just likes the food. Whatever. Maybe the *Crimewatch* shoot is nothing to do with it.

Maybe.

Or maybe he's keeping watch. Maybe he's in some way involved with Lynn Arthur's death. What had Rachel said? "I think Trevor could be dangerous."

Maybe he wants to see what would go out on the BBC. Maybe it's the type of thing that would incriminate him. Am I seriously thinking one of my work colleagues might be a murderer? Well, yes. That was exactly what I was thinking.

I glanced over to Constable Paul Blake, who was probably expecting an easy night watching a TV shoot. Should I say something? At least tell him my suspicions? Suspicions based on what actual evidence? That I thought Trevor was a creep? That someone I'd just met told me to watch my back with him, and that his dead girlfriend looked like me?

Just get through tonight, Brooke. Focus. Don't look at Creepy Trevor. Try to keep your head. Don't let him know you've seen him.

TREVOR KNIGHTSBRIDGE

I'd parked my car in a parking bay about fifty yards from the Pelican Club, and after they'd finished shooting in the restaurant I left discreetly and went and sat in the car. There's something very comforting about the smell of leather seats in a Jaguar. It's a good place to think. Sometimes a long drive helps me to think. Tonight, I just needed the quiet. Trouble was, my mind wasn't quiet. Not yet.

This had been a hard few weeks. Just when I was hoping I could get my life back on track, I couldn't believe my luck when Gemma phoned me and told me I'd got the part I'd always wanted to play. I would have preferred not to have it fucked up by all the crap I'd had to deal with. Well OK, not totally fucked up. But not far off. Been a real exercise in trying to focus on the job.

The film crew had left bags and flight cases for the equipment in the restaurant while they went a few yards along the pavement to film Lynn walking down the road to where the last known image of her was captured on CCTV. I sat there and watched them film it. I sat for about forty minutes. Right. Time to go, Trev. Time for me to be somewhere else. Anywhere else. Anywhere that isn't here.

Except that I couldn't. There was still unfinished business.

Brooklyn. There's something quite special about her and I think I'm the only one who knows about it. Yes, she looks like Lynn. But there's something else. I only discovered it on Saturday night just before the first show, but since then I've wondered more and more about her. That too is partly why I'm here tonight. Not just because of Lynn.

Brooklyn had seen that old guy who turned up on the first night and had sat on the front row. The one Brooklyn had been talking to in the foyer before the show. The man who'd been dead for ten years.

Archie Stephens.

I sat thinking this through for the next few minutes and knew what I had to do. I started my car and slowly did a U-turn and headed for a layby I knew of along the Port St Catherine road.

Towards Forgers Wood.

BROOKLYN

I managed to avoid looking at Trevor the whole time we were filming in the restaurant. Quite a good focusing exercise actually. Might come in useful if ever I'm in a show and there's a psycho in the audience.

Eventually we moved outside into the street for a few shots: me leaving the Pelican Club and walking away from the Seafront down the Port St Catherine Road towards Dunslinton. We'd been outside for maybe fifteen minutes. Mick (or Nick) and Goran were discussing a shot and talking about how the lights reflecting on the wet pavement would give the shot a 'film noir' look.

I was drinking a Styrofoam cup of hot chocolate and sheltering from the drizzle under Josie's umbrella when I saw Trevor. He glanced briefly over to us and then went to where he had parked that Jaguar of his. I don't know much about cars, but Scott had shown me a picture in a magazine of one that looked just like Trevor's and had told me that the X-Type was basically a Ford Mondeo. A fake. *Just like Trevor*, I thought. I saw him get into his car, and just sit there. I knew then that Trevor being there was not a coincidence. That for whatever reason he had come to spy on the *Crimewatch* shoot.

About fifteen minutes later, when we were doing a shot of me walking away from the camera along the neon-lit street, Trevor's red Jaguar drove past, heading towards Dunslinton.

OLD BILL

The Ripple had been flowing today. So Old Bill stayed near where the Bad Thing had happened, and waited. All day. Now it was dark. Normally by now he would be home with the Floppy Clothes Lady and with good food.

During the day there had been people walking, or riding those metal frames with wheels, that humans called bikes. But now it was dark, and especially as Old Bill's eyes no longer saw as well as they once had, he only had his ears, nose and sense of The Ripple to guide him. All his senses were on high alert.

He could smell the person with the Cain Scent.

BROOKLYN

We drove along the Port St Catherine Road for about a mile to a layby from where we would walk the hundred yards or so to the footpath. The night had become quite cold. The drizzle was more like a fine mist. No need for the umbrellas, but the air was damp and each lamppost had its own misty halo.

Ever the since people had been warning me not to walk through the woods, my imagination had turned this place into something from a horror film. Dark. Remote. Scary-looking trees and deep shadows full of devils. Actually, it was just an ordinary path. Quite well lit, and in this section at least, properly tarmacked. According to Josie, a long time ago it had been a railway line. The section where we were filming had a very gentle curve. Goran's idea was to have me walking away from the camera for about a hundred yards until I disappeared from view. This would be the final image of Lynn Arthur. The image which might jog the memory of anyone who saw her on the night she died.

The crew had also brought a small generator with them. The lampposts were due to switch off at about ten. Some local council's idea for saving money, so Josie said. If we needed to, we could film using floodlights powered by 'the Genny' as Mick (or Nick) called it.

***

"Turn over."

"Camera speed."

"Sound speed."

"Slate three, scene one, take one." And the clapperboard snapped shut behind me.

"Action!"

It's only in films and stories told by people who haven't done much filming that you hear people say "Lights, camera, action!" As Rachel had said, once you're there, it's just ordinary people doing a job.

I walked away from the camera and made my way the hundred yards down the path. Once away from the crew, the further I went, the quieter it became. The mist was getting thicker. Goran was quite pleased about that. He liked the idea of Lynn disappearing into the mist as the final image.

I was nearly at the point where I would disappear around the slight curve in the path, when a cyclist passed me from in front and pedalled in the direction of the crew.

"Cut!" yelled Goran from a hundred yards behind me. What a shame. It was a very simple shot, but we couldn't have a cyclist there as well.

A few minutes later we were ready to go again. Goran told me to keep walking once I was out of shot and not to reappear before he yelled 'cut'. So for the second time I walked away from the camera crew. After a few yards I realised that I didn't know the precise point where I would be out of sight from the camera.

Must be nearly there. I kept going.

Suddenly I was no longer alone. The man who surprised me didn't jump out of the undergrowth brandishing a knife. He was instantly right beside me. Not there one minute; right there in my personal space the next.

Archie.

OLD BILL

There were people with things that humans called 'equipment' not far from where Old Bill was sitting. And there was the Young One, walking along the path. The man on the bike had made the Young One stop walking. That had been when someone had made a share thinking noise that sounded like 'kut'.

The Ripple was flowing strangely. The Cain Scent was still there. And close.

I stopped and just stared. Archie smiled that twinkly smile of his. His dark, sharp eyes sparkling in the light from the lampposts.

"My dear, I'm so sorry. I just didn't know."

I understood instantly what he meant. "Archie, I just couldn't believe… what I found out."

"I doubt it not, dear lady. Not for an instant. It was a surprise to me too. I had a bit of a telling-off about it, I can tell you. It was an awfully long time before I could persuade them to let me come back to see you."

I looked at him, and only then did I realise that Archie was *different.* He looked younger. By quite a few years. In fact he looked more like he did in the photograph which hung on the wall in the Institute. No longer the old man in his nineties. This Archie might have been only forty-five, but still recognisably the same man.

"This has been such a weird day," I said.

"How so, my dear?"

"Oh, nothing much. I tried to come and have a cup of tea with you this morning, and then found out you were a ghost! Just a normal day really." It came out sharper than I meant.

Archie looked confused. "This morning? Really? What we used to call 'time' does very strange things where I now live. There it's been more like what we once thought of as a year. Dear me. I'm still getting used to all this. D minus, Stephens, must pay attention."

"A *year*?"

"Something like that. Which reminds me, I need to get back. I came here to make sure you were alright, but also to warn you. This place isn't safe for you. Something in The Ripple."

"The Ripple?"

"It's much too hard to explain. Animals can sense it. Humans lost that sense a long time ago, and they don't get it back on your side of the great sea. Just be careful here, be quiet, be fast, and by the way: next time use the text."

"Use the text?" I said, mystified. Now seemed a very strange time to be giving me notes on the subtleties of playing Shakespeare.

"Just something to keep in mind when you see me again."

And then Archie was gone. He didn't fade away. It was as if I'd looked away for an instant, or maybe just blinked my eyes, and he was gone. Ghosts in real life don't behave anything like they do in stories.

Be careful here. Be quiet, be fast.

I was completely alone. The film crew out of sight. No one in front of me. Dark woods to either side. How long had I been talking to Archie? A minute? Five?

Then off to my left, not far from the path, I heard a twig break.

I moved as fast as if I'd burnt my fingers on an oven shelf. I ran as fast as Lynn's heels would allow, until I had sight of the camera crew. However long I'd been talking to Archie, I clearly hadn't been missed. In fact it seemed as if the crew had only just stopped filming. Like someone had pressed the 'pause' button on reality while I'd been with Archie. Just another little dose of weird in the strangest day of my life. Goran, Josie and Mick (or Nick) were discussing how good the mist was looking, and it was decided that we should do one more shot 'for good measure'.

Once again, on 'action!' I started walking away from the crew along the path. Ahead of me I could see the by-now-familiar arrangement of trees and bushes. Because of the mist, I figured I'd be out of sight of the camera long before then anyway.

I was only a few paces past the point where I would disappear from view, when without any warning, the lights went out and all was darkness.

OLD BILL

Fido was as surprised as the Young One to see The Warm Drink Man. They made share-thinking noises for a while, and then the Warm Drink Man went away. Fido wanted to say hello, but his other senses were on full alert for something else.

After the Warm Drink Man went, Fido heard movement. The Young One heard it too. And ran.

Fido stayed. The person with the Cain Scent was getting nearer.

BROOKLYN

You don't often get full darkness. When you do, you remember it always. This was like someone had come up behind me and thrown a black velvet bag over my head. In the few seconds before things got noisy, there was just dark and silence.

At first, I was too surprised to be afraid. *Be careful here. Be quiet, be fast.*

There was movement in the bushes, a breaking of twigs. Shouts and surprised laughter from the crew. One of them made a joke about needing a shilling for the meter; someone else blamed Margaret Thatcher for privatising the electric companies. Then off to my left, and quite close by, there was a low growl, followed by the deep, resonant, angry barking of a large dog. More movement in the bushes. Someone, or something, struggling through the undergrowth. Someone close to me. I could feel their presence even though I couldn't see them. Whoever it was barged into me, knocking me off balance, and finding my voice, and with a ferocity I didn't think I was capable of, I shrieked, "FUCK OFF YOU BASTARD!" at the top of my lungs. Then there were rapid footsteps running away into the night.

Despite being terrified, somewhere inside I made a mental note that perfectly normal people like me can react savagely when threatened. The sort of thing they try to get you to discover in improvisations at drama school, I was finding out for real.

More canine growling and more deep, well-projected, guard dog-like barking. Sounded like a huge beast. All the horror stories you hear about Rottweilers and Bull Mastiffs were kaleidoscoping in my head like ghouls on a ghost train ride.

"Brooke? Are you OK?" Josie's voice.

"No, not really!" I called back. *Be careful here. Be quiet. Be fast.* Great work Brooke. I had just given away my position to whatever monster was with me in the woods. Failed miserably in being quiet. Couldn't do fast either. No good trying to run when you can't see your hand in front of your face.

The large fierce dog was still barking and growling only a few feet away. Then it was right next to me, nuzzling my hand. *Stand still*, I thought.

Sniffing. Nuzzling, then what sounded almost like a purr, and the dog moved away.

"Brooke, I'm coming towards you shining a torch, can you see me?" Paul Blake's voice taking charge.

There. Through the mist, a small beam of light. Time to *be fast.* I ran as fast as I dared, and the closer I got to the light, the better I felt.

"That was scary," I said, as lightly as I could manage, hearing my voice waver. "Someone barged into me and ran away, and somewhere up there is the Hound of the Baskervilles' evil twin."

"Yes, so we heard. You sure you're OK?" said Josie.

"Yeah… I think so." Then, silly kid that I am, the tears came, releasing all the confused emotions of the day in a sudden rush, while Constable Blake started talking urgently into his radio.

***

I remember a poster I had as a teenager: it showed a girl sitting on an old-fashioned bike with a wicker basket, about to set off down a long road. The caption read: *Today is the first day of the rest of your life.* As an impressionable thirteen-year-old it had, well, made an impression on me.

I awoke the next morning with that in my head, and still trying to come to terms with everything that had happened. Yesterday, which had started with my feeling so excited at going to see Archie and finding out what he had thought of the play, and which had ended with me being stalked by Trevor the psycho and getting totally spooked in the woods, I'd come home to Beth Churchill's, phoned Scott and then gone to bed. But I couldn't sleep. And the reason: Trevor.

So I'd got up, poured myself a glass of wine, watched an episode of *Friends* on my laptop, and then on an impulse, went on to my Facebook account and deleted Trevor Knightsbridge from my list of friends. Just doing that gave me a feeling of empowerment. There was now a limit to how he could spy on me. I started to imagine confronting him when I saw him at work, but eventually I said to myself, *D'you know what? Sod him. Don't let him know he's got to you.* And an underlying thought; *Watch your back. I think Trevor could be dangerous.*

Finally, feeling fragile after a restless night, I went down to breakfast and had my usual big bowl of cereal. Beth was busying around and she asked me about where we were going today.

I said, "We're loading up the van with all the lights and scenery, then we're off to some place near Dorchester."

"And you're coming back tonight, that's right isn't it?"

"Yes," I said. "We've got a few local gigs where we just come back to base, but we're overnighting in Guildford next week when we go to Reading the following day, and then there are a few others like that. I'll give you a list if you like."

"No dear, don't worry," said Beth. "I'm used to people coming and going, and you've got your own key."

That seemed to finish the conversation. Beth carried on with her busying around and I munched at my cereal, then went and got myself ready for the day.

I walked along Sea Lion Street towards the Institute with Old Bill (Fido) beside me. I was ridiculously touched by the thought that this old dog had chosen to accompany me on my walk to work; as though he had been an old man taking his granddaughter to school. Almost as if he was trying to protect me.

I took a few more steps and then the thought came to me like a lamp with a faulty connection flickering to hesitant brightness. The dog in the woods last night. *Really?*

I stopped and looked down at the gentle old dog beside me.

He looked up. Panting.

I bent down and looked closely into those milky eyes. Old Bill sat down.

"Was that you last night?" I said. Partly as a question, and partly as vocalising my thoughts. "What's going on in that doggy mind of yours? What do you know that the rest of us don't?" I stroked the top of his head. He nuzzled my hand.

Just like last night.

I don't know. Maybe last night it had been Fido scaring off a psycho. It kind of fitted. In his strange way, Fido had seemed to be protecting me all the time. Not wanting me to walk through the woods. Always making sure he came with me. It made some kind of sense.

But I was struggling to really believe it. I would never know. It could just be that the fierce-sounding dog in the woods last night was like Bill Sykes' dog, Bullseye. A fierce dog owned by a killer.

Except the dog last night hadn't attacked me. Whoever had been in the woods last night had run off when the dog had made such a noise. And if it had been Fido there last night, barking and growling like the hound of hell, why had he been there at all? Had he been waiting all day?

Yes, he had.

That thought was in my head instantly. I had walked with Old Bill as usual in the morning to Archie's. Archie hadn't been there. But once I'd discovered that, the dog had taken himself off into the woods just like I'd seen him do every day. Except this time without Archie beside him. And later in the day when I'd gone to have lunch with Rachel I'd realised that Fido hadn't come back from that walk. Therefore, he could possibly have been there all day. But why?

I stopped again and looked down at him. He looked up. Emotions from all the weirdness I'd been through yesterday, and the strangeness and terror of last night, started tears leaking from my eyes and my throat feeling constricted. Stooping down, I kissed the top of his head and looked again into those old, faded eyes.

"Thank you Fido. I'm not really sure what for, but I think you were there when I needed you."

We were nearly at the Institute now, and I started to wonder if today Archie would be there, just like before, except would he now appear in the much younger, mid-forties version of himself?

"I wonder what you'll make of that Fido?" I asked out loud. *How would Old Bill react to Young Archie?* I gasped, and stopped in my tracks.

How he would react?

Old Bill had reacted the same way every time he had seen Archie. His whole body had quivered with excitement, he had wagged his tail, licked Archie's hands and had responded to his name: *Fido.*

I thought back to the times when I had spoken to Archie when other people had been there. No one had spoken to him. The time when I'd seen Eleanor Boscombe going through her lines: "Method actress," Archie had said. "So into her part she just looked straight through me."

Fido was my guarantee that I hadn't imagined all this: Fido had seen Archie as plainly as I had. Every time. No doubt about that at all.

Fido walked with me to Archie's door. We stopped. He looked up at me, gave a brief nuzzle to my hand and a light lick, then slowly turned and plodded back the way we had come, without even a glance at Archie's house. Archie wasn't there. Not today.

★★★

There was a curious start-of-term feeling in the cast when everyone turned up. Today was the start of the tour. The first time of striking the set and loading up the van.

It took us an hour or so to take everything to bits and carry it outside. Then there was a lot of hanging around while Keith Groat, who was overseeing the packing of the van, made up his mind where everything should go. It seemed ages since we had unpacked the set that first day, but really it was barely two weeks. And that day when I arrived and…

Archie told me that he had set up the lights.

He had been so pleased at the surprise on my face when he'd told me that he had done it. And that he had done the taped mark-up the day before.

While we were carrying stuff to the van, and when I could have a quick word with him on his own, I said to Derek as casually as I could, "You know when the set first arrived and we unloaded it, and we said that we'd rig the lights the following day?"

"Yeah," Derek replied, looking at me strangely, "what about it?"

"Well, when we got in the following day the lights were rigged and ready to go."

Derek said nothing.

I felt like a little girl asking if the tooth fairy was real. "I meant to ask at the time, but I just wondered who it was who set everything up?"

Derek smiled. "Oh right. Yeah, that was me. Well, me and Groaty."

"Oh I see," I said, trying to sound like it didn't much matter.

"Why?" asked Derek.

"No, nothing, just wondered that's all."

"Yeah, well you and most of the others had gone, then Gemma phoned Jimmy and broke the news about that Rachel not coming back. Me and Groaty were still here and the three of us had a chat about what we were going to do, and the result of that discussion was you getting the part you're now playing. Then because we knew the following day was going to be madness and stress for everyone, me and Groaty decided to rig the lights."

I said, "Ah right, that makes sense." Then taking a gamble, I said, "I never thanked you for doing the mark-up for me the day before either."

"No problem," said Derek, "just thought I'd make your first day working for His Lordship as easy as I could. I'll let you buy me a Guinness when we're on tour."

So that was that. Of course Archie had not done the mark-up, or rigged the lights. Knowing what I now knew, that made sense. Except that Archie had not meant to deceive me. He clearly believed that he had done it, and had been as pleased as a child receiving praise from a parent at my reaction to what he had done.

That was the clue: Archie had believed he had done these things as fervently as a child playing pirates in a play park believes he is sailing the seas in a galleon, or like a little girl playing horses believes she is galloping through a forest. His 'Look, Brooklyn, I set up the lights' was a bit like a little boy saying 'Look Mum, I've been to the South Pole' after playing in the snow.

Meeting Archie was the weirdest thing that ever happened to me. I had talked with him. Smelt the mothball scent on his clothes. I couldn't remember whether I had actually touched him or not, but he had appeared solid enough, not some translucent figure who can walk through walls.

Somehow I just had to accept what had happened, and get on with the job.

***

It was a few days into the tour before Trevor Knightsbridge said anything to me that wasn't hello or goodbye, or what we said to each other on stage.

I'd come to accept that Old Bill had been there in the woods looking after me, even though that idea was still like a fantasy story. I couldn't be so sure about whether the person who'd run off had been Trevor. I turned it over and over in my head:

I think Trevor could be dangerous... Had Trevor been connected with the death of Lynn Arthur?

OK. Facts:

COUNSEL FOR THE PROSECUTION:

1. The guy's a creep. Always watching people. Analysing.
2. He's given me a lot of funny looks.
3. I remind him of his dead girlfriend.
4. He was definitely in the restaurant to spy on the *Crimewatch* shoot and my part in it.
5. He was also watching the street scene.
6. I saw him driving off in the direction we later went to film the woods scene.

COUNSEL FOR THE DEFENCE:

1. Because he's a creep doesn't mean he's a killer.
2. Funny looks? Maybe he fancies you? Maybe you imagined it.
3. Yes, the witness does look like Lynn Arthur. But milord, I refer the court to my earlier point that because my client is, in the opinion of the witness, a creep, that does not make him a killer.
4. Objection, your honour: my client was merely enjoying a meal out on his night off in his favourite restaurant. I would suggest that the witness is the one with a problem and is using my client as a focus for her own insecurities.
5. Once again your honour, I object. My client is a single man who enjoys his own company. He is also a professional actor who likes to watch people for the sole purpose of improving his craft as an actor. He was in no rush to get home that night. He was watching the film shoot as an interested spectator while he listened to a CD on his car stereo system.

My client and I take a very dim view of these damaging and unfounded accusations brought by Miss McCarthy.

6. Objection, your honour. The prosecution has no case. Mr Knightsbridge enjoys driving. His car is his hobby. After listening to a CD after dinner he went for a drive. Yes, he did head towards Dunslinton and Cranton Overleigh to take a more scenic route to where he lives. I should like to ask the prosecution what business it is of theirs which route Mr Knightsbridge chose to take home, and for that matter, did anyone see his car, or him, anywhere near Forgers Wood?

JUDGE: Objection sustained. Do the prosecution have an answer to that last question?
COUNSEL FOR THE PROSECUTION: No, your honour.
JUDGE: Case dismissed due to insufficient evidence.

Trevor Knightsbridge innocent. Brooklyn McCarthy sued for scandal and for being a poisonous bitch.

Headlines in the tabloids:
Young actress accuses Richard III of murder.
Too much into her part.
Go back to the day job, says producer.
Wrongly accused actor tells all.
Exclusive on 'barmy bunny boiler Brooklyn'.

You know those adverts you get on the tube? *If you see something suspicious, report it.* That may be easy if you see a bag or a suitcase that could be a bomb, but it's very different in a situation like this. All I really had to go on was a gut feeling and some funny looks. And who would I report it to? Jimmy?

"Jimmy, could I have a word? You see, well, I don't know how to

put it, but I think Trevor Knightsbridge may be a murderer."

"Well Pussy, I don't know what they teach you in drama schools these days, but I'd given you credit for better character observation than that. I've known Trevor for years. Grow up and stop being so bloody silly."

Not tempting.

The police?

"That's a very serious allegation miss, what actual evidence do you have to go on?" Followed by a long interrogation along the lines of the court dialogue I'd been running in my head. Not tempting either.

Scott. Normally I'd tell Scott everything. But this? When he'd been so cautious about my not walking through the woods, and even a bit wary about my doing the *Crimewatch* shoot at all? He'd probably think it had all got to me too much and that I was cracking up. He might even be right.

Rachel. She who thought Trevor could be dangerous. Yes. Maybe. She was probably the one person I could share a fear like that with. She knew him better than I did, and we'd already touched on the subject over lunch on Weird Monday.

So all things considered, I kept my head down and just got on with the job. Had as little to do with Trevor Knightsbridge as I could. Managed to avoid being on my own with him, and gradually, over a few days, I felt myself calm down; the weirdness and terror of that day fading as the days passed.

Until one day towards the end of that week, suddenly Trevor Knightsbridge was there in front of me.

It was not long before the half. Most of the others were either backstage or outside at the nearby corner shop. Trevor was sitting in the row of chairs in front of where I was. I'd been so much in my own headspace that I hadn't noticed him approaching.

"Hi," he said, "do you mind if we talk for a sec?"

All my defences went to DEFCON 3, whatever that means. "No, OK, if you want," I said, my secret self screaming at him to piss off and leave me alone.

"It's just… Look, I know we haven't exactly hit it off. You and me…" He seemed to be lost for words.

I said nothing, wondering where this was going.

Trevor went on, suddenly looking vulnerable. "OK, fuck it, I'll just say it: I'm sorry OK? I know you saw me that night when you were on the BBC shoot. I thought I'd got away with it, and I didn't see you notice me. But when we got back to work I knew you had. I could tell by the way you looked at me. I must have freaked you out. I never meant to. The reason I was there wasn't anything to do with you, but I just shouldn't have been there. And I'm sorry."

I heard myself say, "That's OK. It did freak me out a bit to be honest."

"Sorry," said Trevor. "My trouble is I'm good at observing people, but crap at not hurting them or scaring them. The thing is… well, as I said before—"

I said it for him: "I look a lot like her, don't I? I mean Lynn."

He nodded. "Yeah, you do. But I still shouldn't have been in that restaurant. I just needed to close the chapter and now I have. I'm really sorry if I put you off your game."

"That's OK," I said, "forget it." And then, to fill what after a second or so felt like an awkward silence, I said, "It can't have been easy for you either. Losing someone you loved." Instantly I wondered if I'd touched a delicate nerve.

Trevor just nodded sadly and said, "People have no idea what it's like. I had no idea what it would be like until it happened, and it's crap. The hardest thing that's ever happened to me. But I'm getting there. Early days yet, but I'm doing it a day at a time. I'm just sorry I made you be part of that without at least... well... asking your permission."

"Really, that's OK," I said. This was not arrogant, testosterone-charged, resonant-voiced leading actor Trevor, nor was this creepy, scary Trevor. This was pensive, thoughtful and vulnerable Trevor, and I began to wonder whether what I was seeing now was closer to the real person.

Watch your back with him. I think Trevor could be dangerous.

I said, "Look, I've probably been a bit off with you too, but if you need to talk about this, or if I can help, just ask me, OK? In the meantime, would you like some flapjack?" I held out my plastic lunch box which still contained a few pieces of Beth's homemade syrup flapjack.

Trevor smiled a friendly, boyish smile (*I can smile, and murder while I smile*) and took a piece. Amazing what flapjack can do. That seemed to break the ice between us and then somehow we started discussing the themes of the play, or rather the themes that Jimmy had brought out in the play: the theme of the curses that Queen Margaret makes against Richard near the beginning of the play all coming to pass one by one, until they all reach their fulfilment at the Battle of Bosworth; and the night before in the 'ghost scene' in Richard's tent, where past events and past enemies come to haunt Richard as ghosts. I think we got onto that through Trevor saying that he'd been trying to 'lay the ghosts' from his own life, and that he needed to remember Lynn without feeling sad. From there we both agreed that Shakespeare had got it right when he'd written that scene where the ghosts appear. I carefully avoided saying anything about how I believed I had met a genuine ghost.

Instead I joked, "Yes, and he even gave a lighting direction. Knew his theatre did Will Shakey."

Trevor looked puzzled.

I said, "It's your line: *The lights burn blue. It is now dead midnight... Cold, fearful drops stand on my trembling flesh* and so on."

Trevor said, "Could be I suppose, but actually that's just a way of saying 'There are ghosts here.' I did wonder about changing the line to make it clearer, but apparently in those days they believed that lights burning blue meant that there were ghosts around. Either that or they discovered North Sea Gas before we knew about it."

I wish I could say that from this point on Trevor and I were friends. But even after our conversation over Beth's flapjack, there were still questions and doubts that hung in my mind like moulding overcoats in a damp wardrobe.

Take heed of yonder dog... look when he fawns, he bites.

Trevor had been in the woods at the *Crimewatch* shoot when all the lights had gone out. I was sure of it. I think. *No, your honour, no actual evidence. No, your honour, I didn't see him. Or his stupid car.*

So why had he admitted to being in the restaurant but not in the woods?

Call it a gut feeling, but something in his eyes told me he was hiding something from me.

Something important.

***

Thursday of our second week, we were in Guildford and were away for the first time on our tour. I'd started to relax into it and to get used to the routine of a typical working day for the Edwardian Palace Theatre's small-scale tour. Usually our call time would be around two in the afternoon at the theatre from where we would travel to whichever hall we were playing, set up, do the show, and then afterwards take down the set again, load it into the van and come home. Usually I'd be home at Beth Churchill's at around 12.30. I would gingerly open the kitchen door and whisper goodnight to Fido, as I'd started to call him, then make myself some toast, pour a glass of wine and then either read or surf the internet until I felt like going to bed.

Today I think we were all quite excited in our own way. Or maybe it was just me. My first ever theatre tour properly away from home, and for the first time on this tour we were playing in a 'proper' theatre: The Yvonne Arnaud. Given that the following day we were going to Reading, the decision had been taken to have an overnight stop near Guildford and set off from there the following day. Jimmy hadn't come with us, and so we all felt like we were being let off the leash.

He waved us off in the van from the theatre and gave us a brief pep talk: "Keep it fresh, do you see?" and then individual notes to each of us: "Brooklyn – yes, excellent work, but keep working that text, do you see? Remember the metre is there to help you. Use the text."

I nodded and just said, "Sure, OK, will do." Another of Jimmy's puzzling notes. I knew what he meant of course. Use the rhythm of the language that Shakespeare wrote. Express the emotion through the language and make the words count. Give the words a tactile quality and enjoy speaking them. All a bit vague and arty if you try and write it down, but it made sense. Once again it was a note to do something I was already doing. Oh well.

Next time use the text.

Archie's words in the woods. What was that about?

I still kept Trevor at arm's length, but we would at least talk. Often about the play.

After the get-in and sound and lighting checks, we were eating sandwiches and a few of us had been chatting in the green room. Finlay went away to run through some of the music, John went out to get a "halfway to decent cup of coffee" and then somehow Trevor and I once again got talking about ghosts of the past.

He said, "We'll see if there are lights burning blue again tonight."

I know he'd explained the meaning of that line to me, but his saying it then; well, I thought it was just Trevor's wanky way of saying 'I hope the show will be good tonight', in the sense of 'I hope we're all really feeling it, and on our game.'

So I just said, "Hope so. I love it when it's like that."

"So do I," said Trevor. "I don't think I'll ever forget that first night back in Cranton Oh. Very special audience that night. Maybe for our first night away it'll happen again."

This was all getting a bit Trevor-weird, if you know what I mean. He looked me full in the face. Dark, sharp eyes boring into mine. I started to feel the adrenalin rush of panic as an intense silence grew between us.

Take heed of yonder dog.

"Anyway… time I was getting warmed up."

And with that, abruptly he went back to his dressing room.

***

After the show we had the get-out down to about an hour. Keith and the two Trevors would usually do the heavy lifting and dismantling of the stage, while Eleanor, John, Finlay and me would between us deal with the lights, screens, props and costumes. Then Keith in the van would call for the various pieces one at a time, which he would load into their designated place.

Rachel had been in the audience and waited afterwards to have a word with the rest of the cast. I secretly regretted saying that I'd go to her place for a drink. It had seemed like a good idea at the time, but now, at 10.40 at night, all I really wanted was a quiet drink in the hotel bar with my touring mates, and then bed in a nice room where I wouldn't have to get up the following day until at least ten. But here she was, and she'd recorded my *Crimewatch* appearance so I could see it and I felt it would be churlish to put her off.

"Guys, I'm going to Rachel's for a swift glass of wine and to see my TV debut," I said breezily after the show.

"Ah, vanity of vanities, all is vanity," said John Murray with a sad twinkle in his eye. When I looked blankly at him he just said, "The book of Ecclesiastes my dear. Chapter One Verse Two." I must have still looked blank. "Only joking my dear. I'm sure you'll be splendid. Have fun." I liked John for similar reasons that I so liked Archie. The unfailing old-world courtesy of a pro who has been in the business for a long time without having become cynical.

"How are you getting back?" asked Trevor Knightsbridge. I was putting on my coat and walking over to Rachel's car. Trevor had been odd tonight. Our talk over sandwiches earlier when he'd gone off so abruptly had, once again, made me want to keep my distance. Well, I was doing that anyway, but you know what I mean.

"Rachel said she'd bring me back. It's only a couple of miles from Godalming to where we're staying."

Trevor looked at me steadily. "I know, but look, she'll have had a drink by then."

I found myself saying, "Yeah I know. To be honest I'd rather come and have a drink at the hotel with you guys. But we arranged this a few days ago and she's recorded the *Crimewatch* thing for me."

Trevor said nothing. The dark eyes looking into mine like an interrogator trying to spot a lie.

I blundered on: "Honestly, it's just a glass of wine and a quick look at a TV show and then I'll be back."

"Look, Brooklyn, you've got my number. If you need me to come and get you with the van then give me a call," said Trevor.

"I wouldn't want to put you out like that."

"Don't be silly, it's only a couple of miles remember?" The dark eyes flashed a smile that was somewhere near warm.

Rachel seemed preoccupied as we walked to the car and I was regretting saying I'd go with her to her place for a 'cheeky glass of wine' and a watch of my TV debut. I thought I liked her, but somewhere in my head a little amber warning light was beginning to glow. After the show finished Rachel waited for me and spoke to some of the cast. She and Eleanor exchanged pleasantries and we had the conversation about how the show had gone and whether she'd enjoyed it. We drove in a strained silence out of Guildford towards Godalming where Rachel had a flat. Despite our lunch date on that Monday, or maybe even because of it, we didn't seem to have much to say. The conversation had all been used up, and we didn't know each other well enough for silences not to matter. I decided that I would have a quick drink, see my *Crimewatch* show and then as soon as politeness would allow, I would make my excuses and go.

Rachel's flat was small but tastefully furnished. I hung around while Rachel went into the kitchen and rummaged around finding wine glasses and pouring peanuts and crisps into some cereal bowls. It didn't feel right to sit down just yet, especially as the sofa, facing the TV, was facing away from the small kitchen where Rachel was.

Beside the TV was a large window looking down onto the street. Rachel's flat was part of a small block, and was on the first floor. Opposite was a street lamp and a few parked cars. I remembered Rachel's comment from our lunch date.

"One night Lynn was at my digs, we were having a girly night in, and we noticed Trevor was outside. Just watching the flat. Sitting in his car."

Suddenly she was beside me, holding out a glass of red wine.

"Oh great, thanks," I said, taking it. Rachel looked nervous and on edge.

"Yes, it is," she said with a slight smile.

"Sorry… yes it is what?"

"Yes, it is this window from where Lynn saw Trevor that time, watching the flat. That was what you were thinking." It wasn't a question.

"I was, actually, yes. How did you know that?"

"Maybe you're more like Lynn than you realise. Always on the lookout." She spoke the words thoughtfully in a way that was not quite critical. I didn't know how to react. Rachel went on: "Parked that dick extension of a car of his just over there."

I forced a laugh. A bit like when you're at school and the teacher makes a crap joke and you laugh because it's polite.

"Anyway, let's get your TV show on the screen." Rachel turned on the TV and busied herself with the Sky remote control. I stayed where I was, looking out of the window.

Then I saw him.

Archie. Standing directly under the lamp post like a detective in some old film.

"Tell you what, would you mind pulling the curtains?" said Rachel.

I was still staring. Too stupefied to answer.

"Brooke?"

"What? Oh yes, sorry, just thought I saw something." I pulled the curtains across, and as I did, I gave Archie the smallest of waves. He waved back and then did something really strange: he mimed opening a book, and reading it. Then he looked back at me. *What was that about?*

"Brooke, are you OK? You seem a bit distracted," said Rachel.

Well, that's a bit rich, I thought, but didn't say. It was Rachel who seemed to have something on her mind. There was a brittle nervousness about her tonight which I hadn't seen before.

"No, I'm fine. Just the play I think. Too many ghosts." For the second time, I was close to telling her about Archie. But not close enough. I sat down on the sofa.

Rachel had pressed 'play' on the Sky remote and was busying herself in the kitchen. Her TV was one of the old sort with a glass screen instead of an LCD one. I was apparently watching the opening of *Crimewatch*, but really I was watching Rachel's reflection in the screen as she poured herself an enormous glass of wine and knocked it back in one go. Then she poured another which she also drank straight down. She was definitely acting strange.

Suddenly there I was on TV. "Whoa! There I am, " I cried.

There wasn't really much to it. The scenes in the restaurant; I felt a bit sorry for the extras. The guy was only seen in a kind of rear profile view, and the woman, not at all. Then we were into the shots of me walking away down the street. There was one brief shot, when I came out the door, where down the road in the mid distance you could just see Trevor's red Jaguar. I stole a glance at Rachel. Hoping, for some reason, that she hadn't spotted it.

Then we were into the final shot of me walking away down the path into the mist. Goran was right. It did look good. Maybe a bit like a 1960s horror film, but atmospheric for all that.

And that was that. Then we were back to the studio and announcements by the presenters, pleading for any witnesses to come forward. That was my TV debut. I was very underwhelmed. It wasn't acting. It was just me wearing clothes and make up that made me look like someone else.

I turned to Rachel who was now sitting beside me: "Thanks for recording it Rachel, but to be honest it's a bit of an anti-climax."

"Pity they cut out the swearing," said Rachel.

"Sorry, what?"

A mirthless chuckle. "What was it? Oh yes, lights out. And then some very unladylike language."

I stared stupidly.

"When that dog started barking, I actually thought the whole thing was a police sting. So I legged it. Nearly knocked you over. Sorry."

I was starting to have what I could best describe as an out-of-body experience. Rachel's words seemed to be coming from far away. As if my ears were hearing them but neither my mind nor my body knew how to react.

I heard myself ask, "That was you? In the woods?"

Rachel didn't reply at all for what might have been twenty seconds. She sat staring into her wineglass. Then I noticed she was crying.

"Are you OK?" I asked.

She spoke slowly, like someone telling you about a disaster

or a serious accident they've seen. Full of truth, but in a simple monotone. "You're so like her, you know. I never should have gone, but I had to see. I knew this time had to come, but without you turning up, I might just have had longer."

I shifted in my seat. I felt like I was in one of those funny zoom shots in a film when someone's really shocked. You know, like that bit in *Jaws* when the sheriff sees a shark attack on the beach.

"She had a way of finding things out you see," said Rachel, looking at me with a distant look. "A bit like a weasel." She paused. "Or a ferret." Rachel's tears were sad, but her voice was bitter. "Know anything about ferrets? They squeeze into the smallest gaps, and once they get their teeth in, they don't let go. Determined. Are you like that Brooklyn? Determined to get your teeth in? Like a ferret?"

Eventually I heard myself say as lightly as possible, "Well, I'm determined to get to bed tonight, so I'll be on my way."

Rachel seemed not to hear me. That flat voice again: "She'd done her homework you see. That Lynn. Ruthless. Just like that brother of hers. Left no stone unturned. Sought me out and pretended to be my friend."

Be careful here, be quiet, be fast.

Time for me to get out of here. I got up from the sofa. Decisive: "OK Rachel, thanks for tonight, I don't know what you're talking about, and now I'm going—"

"BE QUIET!" yelled Rachel with sudden ferocity that startled me and made me sit back down like a schoolgirl made to stay for detention. Rachel's eyes blazed with toxic fire. Then she spoke more softly, while she stared at me like a cat about to pounce. "*Be careful here…*" Rachel looked straight at me for a long time, her eyes never leaving mine as she took a long pull at her drink. "Frightened aren't you? Yes, of course you are.

And you should be. I've not much left to lose now. People in that position do scary things… did you know that?"

"OK," I said, trying to sound like I wasn't about to wet myself with fright. "We can talk, that's cool."

Be careful here… be quiet… be fast. Archie's words in my head again.

Rachel went on, her voice sounding like broken glass. "Just pretending to be my friend really aren't you? Another way you're so like her. Is that what this is? *Crimewatch*? Think you know something don't you? Ferreting around; getting your teeth stuck in?"

My senses were on full alert, and crazily, I was also wondering about Archie. What was he doing standing outside in the street? And what was the charades-style miming of reading a book all about?

"I know that even killing someone doesn't get rid of them," Rachel said, slurring her words. "They come back. The ghosts don't die. They're in your head, in the woods, IN YOUR WORK COLLEAGUES!" She raised her voice to a snarl, which turned into a sour laugh.

Be careful… be quiet… be fast.

"Even when you try to control them, they don't die. They tell you to do that. Think on me, despair and die, despair and die, despair and die, despair and fucking die."

And by the way; next time use the text.

Rachel was still quoting, or almost chanting, the lines from the ghost scene in the play: "Despair and die, despair and die, despair and die, despair and die, despair and die, despair and die…"

Use the text.

"Don't worry," said Rachel. "I'm not going to hurt you, but as you're the one who put yourself up there on TV…"

Use the text. Use the—

"…reminding everybody of what happened that night, it probably means it's game over. For both of us. That would fit wouldn't it?" She laughed and said, "I mean, for fuck's sake, I could even kill the same person twice. Be famous then. Might have done that with the big film job. Never going to happen. Not now. Fucked that up. Thanks Lynn. Now you can FUCKING LISTEN while I tell you how you die."

It was a garbled account, fuelled by quite a lot of red wine, of how Rachel Powell had been in prison some ten years previously.

Text… text… TEXT.

At last my brain made the connection.

I nodded politely while Rachel told her story, and every time she looked away I worked my phone further out of my pocket and onto the seat beside me. Only half my attention was on what Rachel said. The other half was concentrating on surreptitiously sending a text to Trevor Knightsbridge:

Come and get me. Urgent. Danger. Not joking. COME NOW.

I was now very glad that Trevor had been in the habit of waiting outside this flat.

Rachel's story was that she'd been a young and impressionable member of a gang which had committed a violent robbery in South London and had left one man dead. The gang leader had been Tom Arthur; Lynn's brother. He was still serving a life sentence.

Rachel Powell, then known by the name of Rebecca Parnell, been found guilty of being an accessory and had served two years in prison. While in prison, she had turned her life around and had discovered an ability for acting and a passion for the theatre.

Come on Trevor, where are you?

Lynn Arthur, who had hero-worshipped her brother had

tracked down Rachel in the belief that it was she, and not her brother, who was truly guilty of the murder of the South London shopkeeper.

Lynn wanted revenge. Or justice. Rachel, according to Lynn, had got away with it. Lynn wanted justice and compensation for her brother's wrongful imprisonment. Several thousand quids' worth of it. If Rachel didn't pay, then Lynn would make Rachel's true identity known and would destroy her new life as a successful actress. There had also been threats of making her whereabouts known to some of her brother's underworld mates.

At some point during all of this, I became less frightened and more sad. Rachel was a drunk with all the fight gone. The flashes of anger were still there, but no longer vicious.

Rachel had waited one night along the footpath which she knew Lynn would use on the walk to her digs and had hit her hard over the head and then dragged her body into the undergrowth. She had been careful not to leave any DNA-type evidence at the scene of the crime. *Some hope there*, I thought – I'd seen *Silent Witness.*

Occasionally she would look up at me and ask if I understood. Someone who had committed murder was confiding in me as though I were some kind of counsellor. And then, towards the end of her story, she seemed to drift off to sleep.

I just sat stupidly looking at her. Her breathing had changed. She was deeply asleep. I no longer felt threatened, and desperately wanted to leave, but somehow, I couldn't.

The silence was as thick as homemade soup and as cloyingly pungent as urine.

Slowly, I got up. Afraid to wake her. Afraid to leave, in case she died or something, and I'd be to blame.

Come on Trevor.

I went to the window and looked out, just as the driver's door slammed after Trevor got out of the company van.

I waved at him, still afraid to make any noise.

But Trevor wasn't looking at me. He was looking at Archie, who was still standing underneath the lamppost. He walked towards him and they had some hurried words, before Trevor ran towards the block of flats and I heard his footsteps outside the door.

I stayed looking at Archie until I heard Trevor banging on the door and calling my name. I glanced at the door, and then back at Archie.

But Archie had gone.

I opened the door. The dark, sharp eyes registered Rachel asleep on the sofa and then looked searchingly at me. Suddenly I knew what he was going to say, but being me, I had to ask. I struggled to form the words.

"You saw him? You know him? Archie… the old guy."

The dark eyes softened. "Archie Stephens. Yes. I saw him. I know him. I know him very well. Or at least I did. He was my grandfather."

TREVOR KNIGHTSBRIDGE

It all made sense. Rachel leaving the cast when she did had nothing to do with Brooklyn. It turns out she really did have a screen test for a big film franchise. Trevor George has the same agent and told me that story was genuine at least. I'd known about some of Rachel's past. At least I knew what Lynn had told me. I'd also noticed how hurt and confused Lynn was over her brother, Tom. In her very naive way, I think she still saw Tom as a devil-may-care romantic villain. In reality he was a nasty thug responsible for the death of a father of four young kids. What I'd thought had been the start of a lesbian affair between Lynn and Rachel was actually Lynn trying to gain Rachel's trust. The blackmail thing kind of fits. Although I didn't think of that at the time. The hard thing for me to deal with is whether Lynn really liked me. Was I just a way to get her closer to Rachel? That's something I'll never really know. So deal with it Trev, and move on.

I don't know what I feel about Rachel. Part of me wants them to lock her up and throw away the key. Part of me feels sorry for her. She had been trying to rebuild a life she'd thoroughly fucked up when she was younger and then my Lynn, my gorgeous, sexy Lynn, in her childish, stupid naivety had confronted her with her past and wouldn't let it go.

Some things in life leave a long shadow that no amount of name-changing will ever get rid of. The ghosts of the past will still catch up. For Rachel, I suspect they've got her for good. I heard somewhere that once you've been in jail they never really let you go. One little offence and you're back in the slammer. Except this isn't a little offence of course.

I feel quite bad about Brooke. She's a nice kid, and had to face all this crap in her first job just because she happened to look like someone else. Some of that was my fault.

That night when I arrived at Rachel's flat I only had a couple of words with Grandad Archie before going up. I knew it was him as soon as I stopped the van and got out. I had a shed load of things to tell him, and quite a few to ask him. Like what the fuck was he doing back in his theatre on opening night when he'd been dead for ten years? I'd never have used that language of course. He was always so polite. He just said "No time to talk now Trevor, you need to get to Brooke." He looked much younger than I remember him. Brooke had called him 'the old guy', which of course is how I remember him. But this Archie was kind of forty-something. Much younger than I remember him from when I was a kid and Mum used to bring me to his theatre and Grandma Sheelagh would make us tea and jam tarts. Grandad Archie's forty-something face is a bit like the one that looks back at me from the mirror when I shave. I'm darker than he is but the family likeness is there. I take after my mum's side of the family. The Stephens side. The theatrical side. I'm still not sure whether I'll tell Mum about all this. Probably not.

After I told Brooklyn who I was, she burst into tears and then started blathering on about Rachel. Sorry Brooke, you weren't making much sense, and I didn't like the way Rachel was looking as she lay slumped on the sofa. I tried to wake her, but there was more to this than too much to drink. Not long after that I called an ambulance.

Rachel's large glass of red wine had contained several sleeping pills, and the confession that Brooke had been made to listen to had been that of a would-be suicide.

BROOKLYN

That's what happened to me on my first job out of drama school. I'd often heard that small-scale touring teaches you a lot, but I suspect the Edwardian Palace's spring 2014 tour of *Richard III* taught me more than most jobs.

It's a couple of years ago now and part of my dealing with everything that happened, and trying to make some sense of it, has been to write everything down. Until now I've only spoken to two people about Archie. Trevor of course – he and I were so inseparable for the rest of the tour that I think some of the others wondered if we were having a fling. The other person, of course, was Scott who, bless him, has never once told me that I'd been mistaken or was going crazy. Which may have helped me to say yes so quickly when he asked me to marry him last summer.

Trevor Knightsbridge helped with this story. We spent several months emailing each other, often with me apologising profusely for some of the things I said about him earlier on. To make up for it I promised not to edit anything that he'd written but to let him tell his story in his own words. He's become a good friend, and comes to stay with Scott and me when he needs a place to stay in London. He gets on well with Scott, and the two of them drive me mad when they start talking cars and watching *Top Gear* DVDs. Scott now reckons he wants an X-Type Jag like Trevor's and keeps banging on about how the '98 Mondeo on which it's based is such a good car. I dunno. Boys and their toys.

That awful night at Rachel's gave Trevor and me something in common that was unique, and concerning Archie, secret.

A close bond formed very quickly between us, like happens between survivors of a disaster.

The days that followed involved interviews with the police where we each had to make a statement, but after that we just did what actors do: we got on with the job. Rachel was convicted of course. She's in prison. It did cross my mind to write to her, but I haven't yet and I don't think I ever will.

I had a Christmas card from Beth Churchill that year and she told me that Old Bill had died in the November. She'd enclosed a photograph of him taken during my stay there, and in her note on the card she wrote that after that time when I had been rehearsing at the hall, Bill never again took himself for his morning walk. Beth said that was when Bill had started to seem very old. I'm sure she's right. But I think the reason was only partly age. I think most of it was that once Archie was no longer there, Fido had lost a friend.

Archie. The picture by the local artist that Duncan had told me about is in Trevor's house. It shows Archie as I first knew him. An old guy sitting on the edge of the stage, with those piercing eyes and impish smile. Trevor did me a ten by eight-sized copy and I've hung it in the hallway at home, and it's also the 'wallpaper' on my iPad.

As for me: well, I'd like to say I've been fabulously successful and have done the RSC and the National. Not yet, but I'm still hopeful, and things are starting to happen. I did a schools tour later in 2014 followed by a pantomime in the Midlands at Christmas. Then I was back at Baxter Kendrick as a temp, and trying to reduce the boredom of my days by walking around the office corridors every few hours.

In summer 2015 I was back at the Edwardian Palace working for Jimmy Knowles. In the theatre this time, playing a summer season. Eleanor Boscombe was in the company, as was John Murray. One of the plays was *Blithe Spirit* and Eleanor was delightfully eccentric and funny as Madam Arcati. The Port St Catherine summer visitors loved it and the house was full most nights. I was playing Edith, the maid. One night during the last act, I did something I hardly ever do. I glanced into the audience, although to be fair it was more to the side boxes right next to the stage. If, as an audience member you sit there, it can be a bit of a side-on view, but it's not bad. There was Archie Stephens. Sitting in 'his' seat. The one on which Trevor had placed the dedication plaque:

Rest easy Gentle Sir, Enjoy the Show.

Archie was leaning forward with his arms resting against the velvet edge of the box, and grinning away like a child on an outing. Somehow I kept my composure and got through the rest of the play, willing myself not to look over again.

But during the curtain call I did. It was definitely him, his much younger, forty-ish self. He was clapping away as enthusiastically as his hands would allow. Our eyes met. He briefly stopped clapping and gave me the smallest of waves and a twinkly smile. I smiled back, and then looked out into the auditorium for the rest of the applause. When I looked back to where Archie was sitting, he had gone.

I never saw him again. And that was last year. But whenever I play at the Edwardian Palace, and Jimmy has already been in touch with me about next season, I know I shall look over to the stage right box.

Just in case.

AUTHOR'S NOTE

The idea for *Lights Burning Blue* came to me while I was rehearsing for a play in a small village hall in a rural setting which had a pathway leading up to the door and an old cottage next to it. I won't tell you where it is, but it is much as I've described it. In odd moments while I was pacing around outside learning lines or having a break, the story of a young drama school graduate and her friendship with a kindly old man who lived in the cottage began to take shape in my mind.

My thanks to Marcus Fernando, Sally Brooks, Carol Chambers, Margot Turrell and Keith Potts for reading early drafts of the book, giving me excellent feedback on things I needed to change, and for the encouragement that I had written something that others might actually want to read.

Andrew Cullum
May 2015